Kinetikus

The Story of a Divine Lover

Susanne Meis

Orangelily Publications

KINETIKUS-THE STORY OF A DIVINE LOVER

Published by Orangelily Publications Ltd
129 Blagdon Road
New Malden, Surrey KT3 4AN
United Kingdom

www.orangelily.org

FIRST EDITION

A catalogue record for this book
is available from the British Library

ISBN 0-9551663-0-6
ISBN 978-0-9551663-0-3

Cover & Title Illustration by Susanne Meis
Cover Layout by Julia von Strauss und Torney

For Joseph,

my parents, Ute and Peter

and my daughter, Anna

Acknowledgements

I am deeply indebted to Joseph. You are my inspiration and bliss.
Thank you to my beloved parents for their unconditional love and support.
A big angel hug for my daughter Anna. You are my teacher.

I would like to thank Ben Taxy in the US for his constructive feedback on the first draft of K., which encouraged me to add vital sections to the manuscript. A big thank you to Katharine Walmsley for her skilful assistance with proofreading K. I am also grateful to Ian Watson for his valuable general advice. A huge thank you to Julia von Strauss und Torney for her professional support with the cover layout. I am particularly grateful to Christine Harder and Fiona Segel for their first individual reader feedback, and for all the encouragement I received from family, friends and strangers alike.

PART ONE

A Sensual Adventurer

Sandrine loved her body. Moving her hips alluringly, she was absorbed in the music, savouring her dance. Unlike her colleagues, she appreciated most of the male attention she received during her performances. The raw energy of purposeful arousal, beyond any pretence, felt superior to the suppressed desire she sensed from men on public transport. The small round stage, minimally lit, acted as the main light source of the club. Tonight there was the usual crowd, made up mostly of smartly dressed business men, small clusters of younger men with slightly embarrassed faces, and a few unkempt alcoholised louder types. Sandrine had finished her act for the night when her boss motioned her to one of the private booths. Someone had chosen her for a private dance. The first tonight.

*

Approaching the booth, Sandrine was surprised to feel a slight wave of excitement. She had danced for individual customers before but it suddenly struck her that it was a bigger challenge to please one selective customer than a mediocre anonymous crowd. While she had never been concerned about this before, she was suddenly afraid of failure. Realising the absurdity in her need to serve a man she had not even met, she composed herself and entered the booth. She knew the rules - no physical contact but full exposure if she chose. Inside the booth, her eyes quickly grew accustomed to the dimmed lights. He was elegantly dressed and sat in a relaxed manner on the small plush sofa. Nothing in his posture revealed any tension or apprehension - not even excitement. Sandrine was experienced in reading the needs of her customers but was wondering if the man wanted to be aroused at all. Maybe he was new to the club and did not know what it meant to order a private dancer.
Against the rules she broke the silence. 'What do you like?'

1

she asked. Offering her a comforting smile, he breathed in deeply and seemed to look inward for the answer. He was in no hurry. After what seemed an eternity, he said slowly and decisively, '**Dance as if to arouse God!**'

*

She froze for a second. Then choosing a tape with an instrumental piece, Sandrine looked straight into the eyes of the man. The beat of the music began to merge with that of her heart. Closing her eyes, she entered into her own universe. Her arms floating slowly towards the skies, she was dancing for herself, not for anybody else, not even God. Sandrine allowed her body to travel freely with the melody, liberated from the constraints of the mind, into a space of pure movement. Pearls of sweat were forming on her forehead and in the nape of her neck as she stripped down to her under garments.

*

The man observed her with appreciation. Their eyes met for a brief moment and she suddenly understood that he wanted to serve her too.

Sandrine noticed that he had changed position and was now sitting up straight, his hands resting on his lap pointing towards her with open palms.

'*He is receiving my dance with his hands*,' she thought. This was when she first noticed his hands. They were fine and slender. The hands of an artist or musician. She caught herself wondering what it would feel like to be touched by them. Her hips were drawn towards these hands. They began to move on their own like waves lapping onto a home shore. Sensing the heat of his energy field, her mind warned with meagre authority 'No touch!' whilst her soul smiled in victory when she surrendered to breaking the rules for the second time. Her behind nestled peacefully in his hands, as she sat on his lap facing away from him. What perfect hands! So soft, appreciative and receptive. She expected them to move. She desired them to move. Instead *she* began to move. His hands had become an instrument of divine service.

*

Kinetikus had always felt the energy of the unseen. As a young boy he saw the ghost of a king sitting on his brother's bike in his bedroom, staring at him without words, as if he wanted to tell him something about himself. He did not understand then. He was three when he decided that reality would follow his will. He willed his colds away and he willed the universe to be kind to him. But the universe had its own plans on HOW to be kind. People needed to be near him - physically near! When he was eleven, a woman had hugged him innocently and he felt a sudden heat rise in his body, the force of which took him by surprise. He knew that he had sensed her energy in addition to his own. He could feel people in a way that was unique. Often he had taken on vibrations from total strangers and people in the street and felt faint and depleted. Until one day, something unexpected happened.

*

His voice had broken and he had recently discovered an extremely pleasurable way to release energy from his body. He was riding on a crowded bus on the way to school. The bus was old and tatty and aching under the load of the passengers who were battling with the summer heat. Despite the open windows, there was no tangible ventilation and Kinetikus, who was standing up, felt faint. While his right hand was gripping onto a pole, he was trying to distract himself from the heat. He had to survive for another fifteen minutes on the way to school. When the bus stopped rather abruptly at a red light, he felt a pair of breasts bounce against his back. His unusually strong response to female energy had been another of his concerns of late. On the bus, there was little he could do to exchange energy with the clouds. He fought his arousal for a while and then decided to surrender to it. He tried to imagine the shape and size of the breasts of the woman behind him from the way he had sensed them on his back. He could still feel the impact just below his shoulder blades and was forming an image of them. He liked what he saw. A plan formulated in his mind. Casually, he lowered his left hand behind his back. With his palm facing outward, he waited with baited breath for the coming red light to deliver the next piece of his female puzzle. It was not the red light but an elderly lady crossing the road, that rendered the day unforgettable. When the bus gradually hit the brakes, a most feminine treasure was placed perfectly and gently into his burning hand. He could feel his energy pour through his hand into the soft warm mount.

*

He found himself eagerly anticipating the bus rides to school. Every day proved to be an unpredictable adventure. To his endless delight, his hand found many female hips and thighs. Kinetikus grew more and more confident and daring in his puzzle play.

On one particularly rainy day, he was standing on the bus when once more, through a soft fabric, he could feel the shape of the most desirable female organ brushing against his hand. This was an extremely rare event. He instinctively moved closer and, gently, rested his slightly cupped hand against it. Anticipating the usual rather sudden separation that followed either through the movements of the bus or the woman's awareness of his hand, he was surprised when she tentatively moved closer. His heart began to pound and his hand started to tingle with heat which spread throughout his entire body. He gathered all his courage. Very gently squeezing the forbidden fruit, he moved beyond the probability of coincidence. A silent agreement between two people, who did not dare to look at each other, was sealed with the most intimate handshake.

*

The next day, on the bus, his hand was in its habitual place, but off duty, while he was talking to a friend. He instinctively felt a woman approaching from behind. Continuing his conversation, he did not expect his hand to be occupied so suddenly, without his prior consent.
Listening absentmindedly to his friend's account of a family funeral, he found immense pleasure in the ambiguity of the situation. His soul rejoiced as his hand moved on a journey of discovery. He felt a silky smooth fabric and gasped, noticing the deliberate absence of underwear. Time stood still. His blood turned into fire and spread into his loins. Drunken with desire, he realised that there was no obvious way out of his predicament. He decided to disperse the pent-up energy within his whole body. It was spiralling slowly back up his spine when he chose to divert it. He sensed a mighty wave travelling down through his left arm and hand back into the woman. Seconds later he heard a muffled scream of pleasure and felt her trembling in his hand.

*

Sitting in a hotel room overlooking the river, Kinetikus felt tired. It had been a long night. He looked at his watch. 3.07 am. The company he had created out of the ether two and a half years ago was growing rapidly and required his full attention during the day and late into most nights. He

5

loved his work. It allowed him to connect with a wealth of cosmopolitan people and he enjoyed his travels to meet corporate clients. This particular European city, despite its hypocrisy and arrogance, had greeted him with tangible sensuality. It awoke the memory of a previous chapter in his life when merging with the female physical body was all that sustained him. It seemed a lifetime ago. Tonight, in the club, he had submerged himself once more into the old world but with the recognition of familiar pleasure came the scent of loneliness and the desire for growth.

*

He had loved many women throughout his early adulthood. Making love came as naturally to him as his own breath. Remembering the very first time he was granted entry into the female heaven, Kinetikus smiled to himself. Barbara was 11 years his senior and had been one of his most interactive victims on a crammed tourist bus during his holidays. The puzzle play escalated in such a way that fellow passengers protested with righteous indignation. They were thrown off the bus and, suddenly, found themselves on a scorching summer afternoon at the side of a dusty countryside road to nowhere. Two young aroused people being forced to look at each other properly for the first time. He laughed when he remembered their rather brief introductory dialogue. Then Barbara quickly and decisively pulled him under an orange tree where they continued the dance that had opened with a few, not so tentative, steps on the bus. He marvelled at her soft curves and let his hands go on a series of joyful roller coaster rides before her arousal took him to new ventures. Rather than just his hands, he offered his whole body in service, to give and receive pleasure before merging with the absolute.

6

In the beginning Kinetikus was surprised to learn, from so many of these early encounters, that he was the first to end their struggles for fulfilment. Later, he realised, that their pleasure was inextricably linked to the way he could feel and touch a woman. His touch powerfully transmitted his masculine essence, and enabled them to become part of his sensual experience, while liberating their own. They felt his desire, appreciation, admiration and worship of their female beauty, and so saw themselves through his eyes. Experiencing his energy, they simultaneously felt the flow of their own sensuality circulating freely throughout their bodies, while their thoughts were gently pulled into a nurturing black hole. At this void of thought, all they were left with was pure energy flowing through two physical bodies in a loving embrace.

*

With the realisation of his sensual powers had come the greed of a hungry young masculine ego, and Kinetikus, himself, had fallen prey to his prey. He loved the physical union so much that he decided to sample what he perceived as all possible types of women. He started to write down his observations on body types, ethnic backgrounds and appearances, and developed his own theories on how they were linked to the personality and sensuality of a woman. He gained a deep understanding of how a woman's face and body could reveal much of her life-story. Conquering, loving, healing, and befriending many women, he enjoyed his identity of a sensual superhero until one day, he realised, it was merely an illusion.

Kinetikus took his purple notebook and wrote:

My body is a divine instrument of love.

Yet so is my mind and my soul.
I can no longer pretend to love, if all I love with is my body.
To love completely, I have to love with my mind, body and soul.
I now choose to draw into my life the woman who will not only receive the gift of my healing touch but will also bring her unique gift for me.

My body desires to explore, heal, caress and become one with her.
My mind feels inspired, intrigued, challenged and entertained by her.
Our souls recognise each other in the blink of an eye.

Kinetikus leaned back and was suddenly overcome with gratitude:

*I am **feeling** my love filling her.*
*I am **feeling** her love filling me.*
*I am **feeling** our love creating miracles.*

He wiped his tears and continued to write:

With gratitude and certainty, I acknowledge that this precious gift is already reserved for me. With patience, I trust that she will enter my life at the perfect moment. Until then, I will follow my dreams with an open heart and mind, and focus on nurturing myself, while serving others in love and respect.

*

'You are booked on the 10:00 am flight for next week.' His assistant was handing Kinetikus the ticket. He had not been to this grand historical city on business before and looked forward to overseeing the event that he had organised over

8

the past month. His presence was a formality. All the legwork was complete. He would only have to make sure that everything was running smoothly.

'Did you book our usual interpreter?'

'Yes, Mrs. Schubert will meet you at the hotel an hour before the meeting begins.'

'No problem there. Most of the clients speak very good English anyway. We will hardly need her.'

The phone rang.

'Kin, I have got Don on the phone. Would you like to speak to him?'

'Put him through – it's so seldom I get to say hi to him these days.'

*

Kinetikus smiled when he put the phone down. Don was one of his oldest friends. They had shared challenging times together, well before they became successful in the eyes of the world. They had always felt certain of a bright future, regardless of how much money they had in their pockets, and harboured big dreams together. Don had just invited him to his birthday party. Kinetikus realised, that his commitment to focus full time on the business until he could take a backseat, had led to five months of virtually no social activity. Most of his friends knew him to be the soul of the party and were concerned, when he no longer seemed to be interested in women. Don sounded very happy on the phone and Kinetikus looked forward to seeing his friend again, after such a long time.

I deserve a little fun.

The party was already in full swing. Kinetikus was late, which was usual for him, as he liked to make an entrance. There was no point entering an empty party. In the shower, he had thought of all the times that he had ever attended parties in the past. He would usually focus his mind on the type of woman that he wanted to attract. He was always very specific about her body and appearance. He would repeat many times in his mind that he was the most magnetic, desirable person at the party. He would then put to trust that his female playmate would be delivered to him in due course. This was the manifestation game. He challenged the universe with sheer impossible tasks only to be amazed, time after time, to find the embodiment of his intentions heaving in his arms some hours later.

Tonight, he did not feel like a sensual adventure.

I am the creator but I don't choose to experience the same over and over again.

I will change the parameters of the game!

Tonight I choose to meet somebody who can teach me something.

As he arrived at the party, he noticed with amazement that he loved feeling invisible.

Don opened his arms to welcome him.

He took Kinetikus aside.

'You look tired. Are you alright? Have you been working too hard again? You need some serious fun!'

Don gestured with his hands as he led the way forward. 'Let me introduce you to a friend of my sister.'

He pulled him to a group of people and started reeling off names.

Kinetikus was not present. Doing small talk, felt like wading through mud. He was looking for a way to exit the situation. Don had left him with an attractive, friendly and intelligent woman who was absolutely perfect. Everybody could see that…

- Apart from him!

The woman sensed that the conversation grew laboured and asked if he would like another drink from the bar?

'I'll get you one,' he replied happy to have the chance of a change of scenery.

On the way to the bar, he stumbled over something soft in the corner.

He looked down.

It was a teddy bear.

He was puzzled. What was a teddy bear doing in a nightclub? He asked one of the waitresses who looked stressed.

'Natalie, we found Jimmy's bear,' she shouted across the bar to one of her colleagues who seemed equally hectic and hardly took any notice.

'Natalie brought her little boy to work tonight,' she whispered to Kinetikus. 'Our boss is not supposed to know.'

'Where is the boy?'

'Upstairs, asleep in the billiard room. He was looking for it earlier. I have no idea how it got in here.'

Somebody called the girl and she went back to her work.

Kinetikus held the teddy bear in his hand. *I used to have one just like that.*

*

He approached the door, and could hear a child's voice talking softly inside. He knocked at the door.

'Who is it?'

'Jimmy, I found your teddy.'

'Come in.'

Kinetikus saw a young boy sitting on a blanket on the floor of the billiard room.

'I wasn't sure if you were asleep, but I heard you talking to someone.'

'I was talking to my teddy.'

'But your teddy was not here.'

'I know, but I can still talk to him. I told him that he needn't worry, that I am with him everywhere and will find him

11

soon.'

'You were right about that,' Kinetikus smiled. 'I used to have a teddy just like yours.'

'Where is it now?'

'I lost it, and nobody found it.'

'Don't be sad, you can cuddle mine if you like.' The boy continued, 'When I want to find something, I sometimes imagine how it would be if I never found it. First, I hate that thought and get sad. Then I think about all the other nice things around me and that I don't really need it to be happy. I think of my mummy and all the people who love me and, in the end, I am so happy that I don't think about it anymore. And then I find it. Maybe looking for something when you *need* it makes it more difficult to find it.'

PART TWO

Divine Lovers

Kinetikus was flying in his dream. He followed a magic faraway tune. Approaching the music, he realised that it was a voice which was talking melodically in a language he did not understand. He smelled a sweet scent and realised it came from a flower with six voluptuous petals and black spots on the inside. As an orange mist emanated from the flower, he breathed in the voice that came in the mist. He noticed seven big bubbles stacked on top of each other inside his body. They were spinning slowly. One by one, they filled with orange mist and started spinning faster until his whole body turned into mist and completely dissolved.

*

Kinetikus woke up feeling unusually refreshed. His alarm was not due to go off for another hour. He stretched, and decided to go for a slow run to wake up his body fully. He loved waking up with the birds to witness the world asleep. The dawn was crisp and clear. No disturbances from continuously colliding atoms of a rushing nation. *I felt more awake in my dream last night than during the day.*
Running a little faster now, the slight breathlessness was soon compensated with warm blood dutifully being pumped through his lean body. His endorphins had started to kick in. *I am so alive when I feel my body. What a magnificent instrument it is!*

*

In the taxi from the airport, he attuned to the different frequency of this city. *Friendly, intellectual and a lot of troubled history. Cities are like people. This one has been through a lot.* He studied the FT. Nothing particularly inspiring today. His investments looked fine. With the help of a pocket dictionary he practised how to welcome his clients in their mother tongue. The conference would start

15

tomorrow morning at 10.00 am with an introduction by him. This meant he had plenty of time to get acquainted with his surroundings and go over his notes. The hotel had offered him a complimentary upgrade to a larger suite in recognition of the substantial business he brought them. An informal meeting with the managing director of the hotel was scheduled for the afternoon in the hotel lounge. It should take no longer than 30 minutes. He slid the credit card style key through the automatic lock of his suite and opened the door. Something seemed familiar about the suite. He could not quite put it into words but he felt very much at ease in the bright, traditionally decorated, uncluttered space. His window had a direct view of one of the most famous gates in the world. Many people had lost their lives trying to cross the border that no longer existed. *I can still feel it. The divided city.*

An oversized, well stocked fruit bowl caught his attention. He picked a grape and breathed in deeply. What a lovely scent! He turned his head and noticed a bouquet of flowers on one of the side tables.

About half of the flowers were in full blossom. They each displayed six bright orange silky petals which were playfully speckled on the inside. He smiled.

*

The meeting with the Hotel Director had been the usual mix of courteous appreciation for the generated business, trade jokes and a renewed sales pitch. Kinetikus always found it amusing to walk into a first class hotel lobby in a casual outfit, with nobody taking much notice of him, only to be treated like royalty half an hour after registration. *Money seems to buy respect. But it never really does. People can always see the person behind the money. We are unable to hide behind it, but neither should we hide it.*

Money is energy. In its essence, it is pure. My relationship to money reflects how I relate to everything else including myself.

*

Kinetikus was deep in thought and absentmindedly glanced around the hotel lobby, enjoying the buzzing atmosphere that announced the impending evening. *I like big international cities.* To his right, a group of business clad Arabs were talking in hushed voices. *I can see their racehorses win a buck or two at Royal Ascot.* A lively group of 3 women in elegant casual outfits entered the lobby. One of them was laughing loudly when her bright orange coat got caught in the revolving doors. Her laugh was uninhibited and infectious.

*

Kinetikus suddenly felt ravenous. He asked one of the staff members if the International restaurants had started serving food.

'We have two big conferences starting tomorrow and most of the delegates have already arrived. The restaurant started serving about forty minutes ago, and, I am afraid, we do not have any tables left at the moment.'

Kinetikus had learnt to welcome challenges. In his experience, they often harboured the greatest gifts. He reflected for a moment while casting his eyes over the restaurant tables.

'Excuse me, there is a table for six over there with two spare seats at the end. Would you mind asking those guests if I may join them?'

Kinetikus watched, as the waiter approached the table hesitantly, and saw him pointing towards him in an apologetic gesture. *Don't loose the game before I have even*

17

started playing. One of the occupants looked up and Kinetikus flaunted his most dashing, unthreatening smile. *I now choose to eat at this table. I see myself eating at this table. I can taste the food already.* He seemed to have sparked a mini-discussion at the table and heard laughter.

Eventually the waiter, who seemed slightly uncomfortable, came over and directed him to the table. 'They said, if you keep smiling like that, they will have to pay for your dinner too! Apparently you are welcome to join them,' he told him.

Great. He sat down and smiled at his four table mates.

'Good evening. I am Kinetikus, and a very hungry one at that.'

'We can recommend the Thai vegetable curry with cashew nuts, it's delicious.'

'Thank you. That sounds good to me. I tend to trust personal recommendations .'

The group ordered their deserts. *I will definitely have some apple pie with vanilla ice-cream after the main course.*

A lively conversation on the topic of savoury versus sweet endings to a meal ensued. He was unaware that he would not be able to indulge his sweet tooth tonight. When he felt the tingle in his upper lip, it was already too late.

'Oh my God, what happened to your lip? It is all puffy and swollen."

'Really? I am not sure. It stings and feels hot. Maybe it's an allergic reaction to something in the food. It happened to me once before and I was given antihistamines by my doctor. Perhaps the concierge will get some help for me.'

'Excuse me, I overheard your conversation.'

The voice permeated every fibre of his being.

He turned his head and noticed a bright orange coat which hung not so neatly on one of the chairs of the neighbouring tables. She was wearing an orange blouse with sparkly sequins.

'Christina, could you pass me my first aid kit please? It's in my bag under Sonia's chair.'

A little blue box was passed across the table, and she fluttered over to him with a small vial of tiny white pills in her left hand. It read *Apis*.

'Here, pop this pill under your tongue and let it dissolve. Don't talk. Just trust. If there is no improvement or it gets worse within the next 10-15 minutes, we can still seek further assistance. Do you find it difficult to breathe at all?'

'No.'

'Great.'

Her table was being served with food which seemed to consume all her attention in an instant. She started eating.

Kinetikus watched in a daze as she ravished her plate while talking animatedly to her friends.

He waited for a long while.

Has she forgotten about me? It has surely been longer than fifteen minutes?

The stinging sensation has gone, and it feels less hot. I'll check in the bathroom mirror.

He rose from his chair.

'Hey, let me have a look at you,' the orange voice commanded playfully.

'That looks better to me. Much better.'

'One - nil to Homeopathy!'

She made a victorious gesture with both of her fists.

Fumbling for something in her handbag, she handed him a small compact mirror.

He examined his mouth. There was a slight swelling on the left upper lip, but nothing that would have caused an outburst by anybody.

He was stunned.

'I assume, you would like to know a little more about my magic pill?' she asked rhetorically.

Kinetikus breathed in a fruitless attempt to reply, as she continued excitedly, 'Tonight you bore witness to the open secret of your own body's magnificence.'
I only thought of that this morning.
'About two hundred years ago, a German Physician called Samuel Hahnemann developed a natural system of Medicine called Homeopathy. When you graze your finger, the cut will heal with no external stimulus whatsoever in a day or two. Our bodies all contain an inherent intelligence that automatically sets in motion a chain of biochemical reactions to restore and heal itself. In some cases, this healing force does not seem to fully succeed in its task. Hahnemann concluded that something had weakened it or thrown it off track. By administering a specific substance, he was holding up a mirror to the body, making it aware of the imbalance that needed to be addressed. The body could now fully direct its healing force towards the redefined target and heal it with newly bundled energy.

'In your own case, you were presenting with symptoms that were characterised by stinging, swelling and the sensation of heat. The remedy I gave you is called Apis and is produced by the honeybee. If a bee stung you right now, the symptoms you experienced would be very similar to the ones you displayed just a while ago. You might have heard the term: Like cures like.'

Kinetikus' mind was buzzing. *She is like a bee. Does the person who prescribes become the remedy?*

She paused to choose her desert. Orange and Elderflower Sorbet.

He looked at her. Something seemed strangely familiar about her. He seized the moment of silence.

'I was not familiar with the history of Homeopathy. My mother used to give me Arnica and Calendula when I was little, and it seemed to help when I had hurt myself. So, are

you a Homeopath?'
'I am studying Homeopathy, Herbal Remedies and Flower Essences, and love any natural healing tool. A lot are based on the principle of providing energetic impulses, that stimulate the body's own healing resources.'
She looked at him with an intense gaze. 'Do you ever feel the universe is trying to tell you something?'
He looked puzzled. His mind felt intrigued and his body alert.
Lilliane continued slowly, lowering her voice:
'Three years ago, I was a completely different person. I felt stuck in an unhappy long-term relationship. I was unhealthy and bored with myself and life. One day something reminded me of a dream that I had given up on, and I realised that I had to end my relationship if I were ever to fulfil this dream.
'My decision to leave my life-partner caused him and both our families a lot of pain. I had a choice of trying to distract myself from my own pain and confusion but instinctively allowed myself to feel everything that I needed to feel. After a period of intense fear, anger, guilt, shame and lots of crying something unexpected happened.
'Most of the people around me had taken the side of my partner, and either judged me or tried to convince me not to leave him. Yet I had felt an absolute certainty in my need to do so. This inner certainty was more real than anything I had consciously experienced up to this point. It was as if I had been in a deep sleep my whole life. I suddenly realised, that I was truly and solely responsible for all of my thoughts and actions.
'From that moment on, a radical questioning started to happen in my mind. What did *I* really believe in? It did not matter anymore what other people thought or what the generally accepted consensus in society was. I felt totally free for the first time in my life.

'While other people were judging me, I felt deeply inspired. I decided to start looking after myself, focused on my health, stopped smoking and began to jog. One morning, I went jogging and discovered a beautiful old cemetery, which was tucked away behind the park where I usually ran. The sun had just come out bathing the scene in a spectacular light. The old trees were breathtaking, and I had to stop and soak in the beauty of the place. At that moment, I experienced a feeling of being at one with everything. I felt secure, safe, loved and at total peace with myself and my environment. The trees looked as if they were surrounded by colourful light. It was as if my perception had changed. My senses were sharper and I could smell, hear and feel everything around me in a previously unknown way. Colours looked bright and intense and I felt energised.'

I know this feeling. I know what she is talking about.
Kinetikus heart started beating fast.
She was slightly breathless and her face was flustered with excitement.

'After this experience, the coincidences in my life grew almost exponentially. They reached a level at which I was doubting my sanity. I felt more awake than I ever had in my life and wanted to shout out to strangers on the street to wake up.

'Luckily, at that point, I met somebody who could explain what had happened. I was browsing in a bookstore, and a man and I simultaneously grabbed the same book. We laughed. He said that he could see my energy field and was a doctor from India, currently writing a book on coincidences. I was suspicious at first but soon realised that he was genuine. I was desperate to tell someone about the coincidences that had happened to me. He seemed very familiar with my observations, spoke about his passion for Energy Medicine and first introduced me to the basic principles of Homeopathy. I felt inspired to find out more, and about a month later after I had devoured over 10 books that were relating to Natural Healing and Growth, I decided to change my career and study Energy Medicine.

'Do you remember when I asked you if you ever felt the universe was telling you something? I have personally experienced two different types of coincidences. One is the type of coincidence where you have a question, thought or intention, and in what seems an impossible or improbable time, you witness the manifestation of that intention. For example, the most common one that people have experienced is thinking of calling someone and receiving a phone call from that person seconds later. Or, in my case, I frequently look up a word in a dictionary or phonebook and open the right page straight away. Whenever I ask myself a question, I get the answer usually quite quickly.

'For example, I was sitting alone on a train returning from my college and was wondering about a movie I wanted to see in the cinema. I asked myself if it was still playing in the theatres. About a minute later, a couple sitting to my right started to talk about exactly that movie. "The cinema is only showing it for another week," the man said to the woman. "Let's go and see it tomorrow night."

'This type of coincidence I understand as a sign that I create my reality. I am the one that has manifested this situation. It is a totally mind blowing concept but I have had enough references to come to the conclusion that there is no reality apart from the one we create at any given moment. These are what I call the pseudo coincidences. Because, of course, there are no coincidences at all. It's simply cause and effect.'

I did it every time to attract a specific woman but never really thought about the mechanics.

'The second type of coincidence is really just a playful reminder of the first. Have you ever noticed that some people, circumstances and situations seem to run parallel to your life. It is sometimes referred to as synchronicity. For example, I found out that Dr. Samuel Hahnemann was German. He used to be a translator before he developed Homeopathy. He was born in a town called Meissen and is buried at one of the most famous cemeteries in the world, the Pere Lachaise, in Paris. Now, I am German, I worked as a translator before studying Homeopathy, my family name is Meissen, and ten years ago I lived in a house in Paris that was literally overlooking the Pere Lachaise. In fact, I found numerous old photos I took of the cemetery because I was fascinated with it at the time.'

She leaned a little closer, laughed and declared loudly: 'Now, that is the universe winking at me unashamedly saying "YES, YOU ARE ON THE RIGHT TRACK GIRL, YOU ARE NOT DREAMING! " '

Kinetikus took a deep breath in, looked at her and sighed.

'You speak my language!' he said.

*

Kinetikus looked at the small piece of laminated orange card in his hand. It read "Lilliane Meissen - Linguistics, Art, Energy Medicine" followed by a phone number and e-mail address. He poured himself a drink from the mini-bar and tried to remember her face. Was she attractive? He did not know. How strange not to remember anything about her appearance. All he could remember was her voice. He could listen to it forever. His mobile phone started vibrating in his pocket. He had put it on silent mode in the restaurant.

'Don! Hi! How are you?' Kinetikus was delighted to hear his friend.

'I just wanted to catch up with you. You left the party rather early? '

'Don, I have to tell you something.

24

'I just met somebody very special. I feel that she will be extremely important to me. Maybe we are supposed to work on something big together. She is unlike anybody else I have met. It was so easy to listen to her. She talked about things which, I realise now, I have always known but could not put into words.'

'Hmm, you don't seem to make much sense. Is she attractive? How old is she?' asked Don.

'I don't really remember how she looks. I believe she is of a similar age to me. I really enjoyed her company and the hours flew by. It felt, as if I was in a bubble when I was listening to her. I don't remember anything that happened around us. Her friends must have left the table at some point because, at the end, there was just the two of us left and the waiter politely asked if we wanted the bill. She gave me her card and said that she really enjoyed being able to talk non-stop about her pet-subjects. I will call her tomorrow to see if we can meet again after the conference.'

'Sounds intriguing. Keep me up to date on this, will you? I am still waiting to meet my mystery lady and can always do with some tips," joked Don.

Kinetikus did not feel like continuing the conversation. He wanted to reflect on the evening without having to explain himself. *I don't myself exactly understand what has happened.*

*

He had two missed calls. His assistant had left a message to let him know that Mrs. Schubert was unable to interpret for him at the conference and that the agency was trying to find a last minute substitute to fly out the same day. The other phone call was from the translation agency. The message was: "Thank you very much for trusting in our services. We are delighted to inform you that one of our top former freelancers was willing to fly out today at very short notice. Miss Meissen will arrive at about 7.00 pm tonight and will meet you at 8.00 am tomorrow morning for a briefing in the lobby.

He laughed out loud. *She lives in the same country as me, possibly even the same city and, now, she comes here to interpret for me. Now there's a COINCIDENCE.*

*

'Looks like you are about to save me for the second time.' Kinetikus smiled at Lilliane who was waiting in the lobby with a big grin on her face.

'When I heard your name last night, I thought it sounded familiar. Only when I looked at the fax from my agency this morning, did I realise that I was here to work for you. Isn't it amazing, while we are talking about coincidences, the universe is having a really good laugh?'

'Would you like a coffee? Have you already had breakfast?' Kinetikus asked.

'Thanks. I'll just have a herbal tea please.'

He ordered two teas and a Danish pastry for himself.

Kinetikus was relieved to see how easy it was to talk about the conference and the schedule for the next two days with her. She suggested a small organisational change that would save him time and save the company money, while serving the interests of the conference delegates. He was impressed. *It is so easy to work with her.*

*

Kinetikus had finished his introductory talk and the delegates began the first series of breakout sessions in five different rooms. He had to speak to the technical company about the afternoon and evening presentations in the ballroom. Mr. Kirschner did not speak English very well and Lilliane was grateful for her first opportunity to assist. Kinetikus told her about the final details of the technical set-up. They had previously discussed the specifications for the stage and the presentation screen but Mr. Kirschner wanted to know if Kinetikus had any preferences as to what colour the background of the stage should be lit.

When Lilliane began to speak in German, Kinetikus went pale. A shock of recognition surged through his body. Her voice.

He looked at her. She was wearing an orange trouser suit with a white blouse. *I dreamt of her voice before I even met her.*

He excused himself to get some fresh air.

*

During the lunch buffet Lilliane joined him.

'I am having fun,' she said. 'We have decided on orange and purple for the lights. Orange for the afternoon session and purple for the evening session after dinner. The screen is amazing. I always find it fascinating to see what goes into organising these events. It's one of the biggest back projection screens I have seen. The ballroom is lovely of course. Chandeliers and the lot.' She smiled at him. 'I also arranged for some more cordless microphones. They are always useful for audience questions after the presentation.'

He looked at her. 'Why do you wear so much Orange?'

She smiled inwardly. *I dress in the colour of my favourite flowers. Orange Lilies.*

Kinetikus sighed. *I should have known.*

*

Kinetikus decided to do what he knew he did best. To simply go with the flow. He stopped wondering, why he had dreamt of Lilliane, and just relaxed and enjoyed her presence. The conference had gone extremely well. People congratulated him for his excellent work. Kinetikus noticed, that most of the positive feedback he had received, included reports on Lilliane. Some people seemed to believe that they were business partners. *It felt as if we have been working as a team for a long time.*

*

The delegates had all left. Kinetikus and Lilliane were now standing in the hotel lobby near the revolving doors, where she unwillingly had made her first impression on him. *It seems like an eternity.*

'When is your plane leaving?' she asked.

'In about three hours.'

'Looks like we are on the same flight,' she chimed.

'I am not surprised.'

'Neither am I.'

'Let's meet in the lobby in an hour. We can share a taxi to the airport.'

'Good idea. I would love to talk more about the conference.'

*

A large orange travel bag occupied the boot of a taxi. It was travelling with a very stylish black suitcase and enjoying the ride.

*

Kinetikus and Lilliane entered the airport.

'Lets check in together,' said Kinetikus, 'I have not yet had a chance to thank you properly for all your help.'

She smiled. *I was hoping he would suggest that.*

He very discreetly upgraded her to business class.

When they arrived at their allocated seats, she whispered to him, 'You know they made a mistake here, I am not supposed to be in business class but I am not going to be the one to tell them. If nobody complains, I'll stay put. I have learnt to accept the gifts of the universe.'

I am the universe, he thought.

'Tell me about orange lilies,' he heard himself ask.

She hesitated and looked at him, as if searching for something, and eventually replied, 'My first ever lecture on Flower Essences, introduced me to orange lilies. Flower Essences are beautiful remedies that, similarly to Homeopathy, will give a safe natural energetic healing impulse to the body. My favourite Essences were developed in Alaska. They include Gem Elixirs and Environmental Essences, and transmit one of the most pristine energy that is available to us. They are simply divine.

'At this first lecture on Flower Essences our teacher had brought a big bunch of colourful mixed flowers to the classroom. She invited us to each pick one flower that somehow spoke to us. I was apprehensive at first, as I did not think any flower would speak to me, in any way. However, the first flower I noticed, was a single stem of orange lilies and, to me, they seemed the most beautiful flowers in the entire bunch. I waited eagerly to see if somebody else would choose the flower before me. But to my surprise everybody picked a different flower. When it was my turn to choose, the orange lilies were still available.

'We then simply looked at the flower in our hands, closed our eyes to feel its energy, and allow any thoughts or feelings in connection with it to rise. When I looked at it, I thought it was the most beautiful flower I had ever seen. I noticed the intensity of its bright colour and closed my eyes. I felt my hand tingle and my eyes well up with tears at the realisation that the flower and I were one. I was looking at myself. My beauty, my potential for growth. Most of the blossoms had not opened yet but the single stem contained many more closed buds. I felt overwhelmed with gratitude. Later, it suddenly occurred to me, that my name also carries the flower in it.

Lilliane, of course.

'And the most amazing thing is that, since that lecture, orange lilies keep popping up in my life. It's as if, at that moment, my personal sign language with the universe was established. Whenever I am feeling a challenge, have chosen to act out of love, or in spite of fear, somehow orange lilies show up. To me it's a sign of being supported on my path.

'For example, once I made time to visit a friend in hospital. When I entered her room, I was thrilled to find that the wall facing her bed was adorned by a beautiful painting of orange tiger lilies and white water lilies, which are her favourite flowers. We were astounded to notice that in addition to the print, the curtains in the room were teaming with huge orange lilies.

'Another time, I was in a park and a little girl of about three sat down next to me on a bench. Her white dress was full of orange lilies and she turned to me and said with a cherub smile, "Hello, my name is Lily! "

'I feel we all have the chance to receive support communication from the Universe. We simply have to choose our individual signs and be completely open to the magic of receiving messages in this way.'

Lilliane looked at Kinetikus.

He sensed that she felt vulnerable sharing something of such deep meaning to her.

"That's beautiful. I have never thought of the possibility of a connection with a specific plant or flower but have felt very connected with nature many times. I love sitting under big old trees.'

They fell silent for a little while. It felt safe.

Lilliane opened her eyes. The plane had touched down. Kinetikus was observing her. *How long has he been looking at me?*

He smiled at her. 'My favourite colour is purple.'

She nodded sleepily.

He suddenly seemed a little restless.

'Lily, I would like to meet you again.'

He called me Lily.

'I have really enjoyed your company, not to mention that, without you, I might still look like a boxer after a fight and the conference would have been a disaster. Thank you so much for all your kind help.'

'You are very welcome, I had a fabulous time.'

He took a deep breath. 'My company has recently opened new offices, and we are having an informal reception in two weeks to celebrate our achievements. Do you have any plans for next Friday? I would love you to be my guest.'

*

The next day Lilliane was on the train from her college when her mobile phone rang. She saw that it was Kinetikus.

'Oh hi, I am on a train and can't really talk now but I will be home in half an hour. You can call me then.'

Kinetikus put down the phone. He felt a little uncertain. *Did she not want to speak to me? Is she really on a train/? She did say to call her in half an hour. I guess it's a good thing that she would like to talk to me in a more comfortable environment.*

Lilliane put her book bag down and threw off her coat. She had rushed home and was waiting. She had forgotten what she was waiting for until the phone rang.

She picked it up. 'Hi Kinetikus, I hope you did not think I was rude to cut you off like that. I like taking my time when I talk to people and I don't like conversations on public transport.'

He felt relieved.

'I think it's great that you wanted to take your time to talk to me properly,' he laughed.

'I thought you would probably have a very good reason or wanted to hire me again.'

He did not.

'Actually, I had no real reason to call you. I just felt like talking to you.'

Lilliane felt a little uncomfortable. 'I guess there is nothing wrong with that.'

She hesitated. 'I feel I can be totally honest with you. I can not remember the last time it felt so easy to talk to somebody. I enjoyed our conversations and your company more than anything else. At the same time, I am having a really good time getting to know myself at the moment. I have many dreams, projects and studies that I currently focus on. Energy Medicine is only one of them. What I am trying to say is that I don't want you to get the wrong idea as to how I feel about you. I would love to know you as a friend.'

Kinetikus felt slightly confused. All he had wanted was to talk. He had not thought about why or how. Most of the time he followed his instincts. He did not feel the need to give a conversation a label. His ego felt a tinge of disappointment, while a much bigger part of him continued to celebrate.

'Well, I am glad we got that one out of the way,' he laughed.

'Now we can have a superb chat like two girlfriends, if that's OK with you.'

Lilliane felt relieved.

Doesn't he find me attractive at all?

'Tell me about the project that is most on your mind right now?' Kinetikus asked.

Lilliane laughed. 'I recently entered a charity fundraising challenge. I have committed myself to raising the necessary amount of money to enable a disabled child to buy a customised wheelchair. If I am successful in raising the money, the group of fundraisers will celebrate their achievements on an adventure hiking trek in China. I have never been to China before and I have never done much trekking or hiking either. To me, it seems like the perfect double challenge. One is the mental challenge of raising the necessary funds and the other is getting to know my body under extreme conditions.'

'I guess, I am interested in testing my limits. Maybe I need something to put me in my place, after experiencing that I have no limitations at all.'

He smiled to himself.

'I have learnt so much already trying to raise the money. I expected it to be a little easier,' she sighed. 'At the moment, I am organising a fundraising party and am looking for a venue. I know someone in a band who has offered to play for free and I've got a massively reduced "sale or return" deal with a drinks wholesaler. Pretty much the only thing that proves a challenge is the venue. All the places I've looked up have horrendous rates.'

Kinetikus interrupted her. 'You might want to get in touch with your local charities and ask them where they normally hold their events. They probably also need to keep costs down to a minimum to raise the maximum funds for their causes.'

'That's an excellent idea. I will make some phone calls tomorrow.' Her spirits lifted instantly.

*

Kinetikus put down the phone. He felt light and happy. He looked at the time. They had been talking for over two hours. He loved listening to her. She was so passionate about life. He was really looking forward to meeting her again at his office reception.

*

The kitchen timer was bleeping. His pasta was ready. Kinetikus loved to cook. He strained the pasta and dished himself some of the vegetable sauce. A tomato salad had already been soaking in some olive oil, lemon, garlic and fresh basil for a while. The phone rang. He let it go to voice mail.

'Hi, it's Lilliane. I just wanted to tell you the good news. I found a great place for my party. Thanks so much for your advice. Emm, if you'd like a chat and are in later, feel free to call me. I usually don't sleep before midnight anyway. Otherwise see you next Friday at the party.'

Kinetikus felt as if he had company during his meal. It tasted better than ever. He ate slowly and enjoyed having to wait a little longer.

*

Lilliane knew that it was him before the phone started to ring.

'Hello.'

'Hi, I hear you have some good news for me?'

'Oh yes, you won't believe it, I found a super place. Guess how much it will cost me for the entire night? It's a very nice hall which holds about 200 people. There is a decent stage and a bar that we can use.'

'Fifty pounds would be a superb deal for a venue like that.'

'Only 10 pounds!'

'Really, that's amazing. Where is it?'

'Not far from where I live. It's a hall that belongs to a church. The church hires it out to charities at very low cost to support good causes. The woman I spoke to was really nice and it only took three phone calls to get her contact details. I have booked the hall for the second Saturday next month and

34

I am inviting over 200 people. I've spent most of the day sending invitations via e-mail and designing the tickets. Do you think you can make it?'
'I'll have to check in my diary but I wouldn't want to miss it for the world.'

*

Lilliane felt very excited. She had not been to an event like this for a long time. She was wearing one of her favourite tops with a black skirt and orange boots. The top was a shiny fabric in orange and purple mixed in a funky pattern. It emphasised her female curves. *Am I dressing like this for him or myself?* She took a deep breath in. *I really do love parties. How exciting not to know anybody apart from the host. I wonder if he will have any time for me? Whatever happens, I am going to have fun.*

She smiled and confidently opened the door to the offices. The entrance area looked very stylish. Lilliane could hear music and voices coming from the back.

Kinetikus looked a little tired but very happy to see her. He took her coat.

How could I possibly have overlooked her appearance?

Lilliane noticed being noticed and enjoyed the attention. She was offered canapes and champagne by a waiter. *What a great place!* Kinetikus was soon surrounded by well wishers and looked a little distracted. She could feel his gaze on her at times and enjoyed the knowledge that he would rather talk to her. It was fascinating to talk to some of his friends. A couple of people seemed extremely curious about her. *What has he told them about me?*

She was chatting to a group of people when Don approached her.

'I hear you made quite an impression on my friend,' he teased.

35

She did not take the bait. 'You must be Don. Kinetikus has mentioned your name to me. I would love to see his office. Can you show it to me? The man himself seems rather busy?' 'Sure, follow me.' Don seemed happy to be of service.

They entered a spacious modern open-plan office with many desks. *I like the fact that he chooses to have his desk in the same room as his employees.*

She looked around and suddenly knew exactly where his desk was.

She stared at the wall above the desk until Don asked her if she was alright.

'I guess this is his desk,' she sighed.

'How did you know that? They are all the same.'

'The painting above his desk – I have exactly the same in my living room. It's almost completely in orange, my favourite colour.'

'I think he bought the print when the new office opened, just before you met him.'

She noticed Kinetikus approaching. 'Here you are! I was afraid you felt completely abandoned and had left the scene of the crime,' he joked.

I felt connected to him all night, even when he was in a different room.

'I have just discovered our mutual taste for modern art. Can you believe I have the same print hanging above my fire place?'

'Is this the first or the second type of coincidence?' he teased.

*

Lilliane was waiting again. The phone rang. She felt disappointed, when it turned out to be the wrong number. She debated whether to call him. It was very late.

The phone rang again and she blurted out, 'I am so glad you're still up. I had a lovely time at your party. Great

offices. I am impressed. I am slightly annoyed though. Every time I look at my painting, I have to smile. Now I am smiling permanently and find it hard to concentrate on my books.'
She paused.
Silence.
'Hello?'
'Kinetikus is that you?'
She heard a squeaky artificial sound, followed by a high pitched male voice: 'Milady, this is the Guinness Book of Records office, Congratulations! You have been entered in the "Speaking without Breathing" section.' She heard laughter. It was Kinetikus.
'How were you sure it was me?' he asked.
'I just did.'
'How are you?'
'Actually, not so good. I feel really stupid.' She remembered what she had been trying to forget all day and felt tears welling up. *I am not going to cry on the phone to a virtual stranger.*
'Why? Do you feel like talking about it?' *In her case a purely rhetorical question.*
'I thought, I had a brilliant fundraising idea, but it was the most humiliating experience of my life.'
'Come on, it can't be that bad.'
"Please don't laugh at me.'
'Would I ever do such a terrible thing?'
'This is serious.'
'I am listening.'
'A couple of weeks ago, I organised some collecting tins for my fundraising. I had been collecting donations outside supermarkets and also door-to-door in the evenings. I got some good results.'
'That's great.'
'Yes, but suddenly I had this idea. I knew from funfairs I had

37

visited that people there collected money for charities. I remember seeing one of these fundraisers give a sticker and peck on the cheek to each donor as they made a donation. It felt perfectly innocent. Anyway, I got this brilliant idea of selling "kissograms". A pound for a lipstip peck on the cheek. I got greedy. I could literally hear the pounds filling the tin. I imagined a friendly family atmosphere with kids, everybody willing to contribute to a good cause, and Grandpa happy to get a peck on the cheek. How on earth I thought it might be nice to kiss total strangers, I really don't know now.'

Kinetikus was beginning to form a picture in his mind. *I am glad she can't see my face.*

'It gets worse,' she sighed. 'I asked two good-looking friends of mine to help me out on this harebrained scheme. Somehow, I convinced them that it was a good idea. I can be very persuasive, you know.'

Yes I do.

'I called three publicans and got permission to visit their premises. I guess, they thought I was a little crazy! We dressed to kill and set out a little later than we expected. Nearing the entrance to the first pub, I got this terrible sense of impending doom but I did not allow my ego to listen to my instincts. Entering the pub with a not-so-brave smile and my yellow collecting tin, I am clearly visible to everybody. The owner recognises me and waves encouragingly as if he knows what torture lies ahead of us.

All I can see are old, unshaven, beer-bellied, smoking, lonely freaks. The girls look terrified. I lead them into disaster shouting: "A peck for a pound. It's for charity." The guys start grinning as if Christmas has come early. We begin our dirty work. I can hear someone asking one of my poor friends if she can kiss his dog. The worst thing is that I dragged my friends into this. I feel so ashamed.'

Kinetikus sensed that she was close to tears.

'I never ever want to kiss anybody again,' she sobbed.

We will see about that. He felt he needed to let her cry fully.

Lilliane stopped crying after little while.

'I feel much better already,' she sighed.

'I definitely learnt something from this,' she said. 'In the first place, I will trust my instincts more in the future. Second, it's just not worth trying to trick people into giving you something. I assumed that they did not want to give freely for a good cause, that there had to be something in return. I guess if I expect only the worst of people that is what I am going to get. I did not even give them a real chance to contribute. I bet some of them felt just as bad as I did. Who wants to pay for a bloody kiss anyway?'

Her sadness turned into frustration, and Kinetikus had a strong inclination that it would all end in laughter.

'May I ask how many units you sold?' he inquired with a smile in his voice.

'I sold fifteen. The girls collected twenty-six between them.'

'Half an hour of hell brought me £41 closer to China.'

'I think we should celebrate your achievements.'

'What?'

'I am serious. It's important to reward yourself.'

'Rewarding for *what* exactly, making a *fool* of myself?'

'Well, you did achieve a measurable result in the form of £41 towards a child's wheelchair. It might not have been by the most pleasurable means, but then a lot of great people suffer for good causes.'

'I doubt if Mother Teresa would have sold kisses," she giggled.

'Everybody makes mistakes but not everybody learns from their mistakes. That's your real achievement. Congratulations!

I will think of something we can do to celebrate, and call you tomorrow at the usual time.'

'Do we have a usual time?' *He must be joking.*

'Well for the past two weeks, we have called each other every two days at around 10.30. Today was an exception with 11.30.'

'If you call me tomorrow, you would mess up our well established pattern,' Lilliane joked. *I am not addicted, I don't have an addictive personality.*

'We can start a new pattern. What about twice daily?'

'You frighten me.'

'I am terrified of you, too.'

'We have got so much in common.'

They laughed.

'Kinetikus, it's really really good to talk to you.'

'I know.'

*

She entered the lobby of the small, classy hotel where she was meeting Kinetikus for their celebration lunch in the French-style Brasserie. He had not wanted to disclose to her what they would do after lunch but sounded excited on the phone. It was Saturday and, in the evening, she was invited to a party by the drummer of her fundraising party band. Kinetikus sat at one of the round cast iron tables and was reading. He saw her approaching and put down his book.

'Hi, have you been waiting long?' *I am glad he was here first.*

'No, maybe 5 minutes. It's hard to believe we've only met on two occasions before.' *It's as if I have known her forever.*

'Yes, but then, we have been on the phone quite a bit.'

She grabbed a menu, and seemed to be delighted with the choice of food.

'This is our first proper meal together,' she said. *It's not a date, just two friends having lunch.*

'Why don't you tell me what we are doing after lunch?'
'Don't you like surprises?'
'Yes, but only the ones that I like.'
'Well, I know you will like this one.'
'Great.'
Lilliane seemed a little less talkative than usual.
'I just love this kind of atmosphere.' She was taking her environment in although her silence did not last for long. 'I did not know that there were places like these around here. It's great. The old world charm, shabby chic, countless paintings in chunky gilded frames, French chansons and a waiter who treats you like royalty. You certainly don't get that in Paris,' she laughed.
Kinetikus smiled. He enjoyed observing her expressions.
'I love watching people,' Lilliane continued. 'Do you think that's rude?'
'No, not at all, it's natural to be curious and interested in other people's behaviour. Ultimately, we are interested in seeing aspects of ourselves. I find, I can tell a lot about a person just by the way they carry themselves.'
'I think the woman over there is an actress from a James Bond movie.' Lilliane was excited.
She whispered, 'She is very beautiful, don't you think?'
'I am sure most people would say she is attractive by normal standards.'
'Yes, but do **you** find her attractive?' Lilliane asked.
'I can see that she has got a symmetrical, defined face with pretty features and a feminine body but I do not feel attracted to her.'
'What do you find attractive in people?'
'When they are happy and comfortable in their own skin.'
'But, surely, you also like someone to look nice?
'I have met a lot of beautiful women and got bored quickly with many of them. They treated themselves like objects and

became very frightened, when I did not do the same.'

'That only shows you are different to most men. These women were not used to being treated like humans.'

'If you think you are an object and treat yourself like one, others are likely to do the same. A lot of men have fallen into the same trap and feel treated like objects by women too.'

Kinetikus continued, 'You end up with two people who are interacting from a place of fear. Fear of being judged. This leaves no basis for honest communication. They don't have a real chance of getting to know each other if they don't allow themselves to be who they truly are.'

'I can be totally myself with you!' Lilliane said quickly.

'You have to know *how* it feels to be yourself first. You have to be yourself with yourself before you are able to be yourself with another person. That's the hardest part for most people.'

'I have been practising for about three years now,' she said proudly.

I have been practising for most of my life, Kinetikus thought amused but chose not to express this particular thought. *She is so adorable in her enthusiasm.*

'There was a time' Lilliane continued, 'when I did not know at all who I was. This was followed by a time when I became aware that I had not been myself. I am grateful to have gone through these phases as they helped me to truly appreciate the difference between now and then.'

He wondered if *he* had truly appreciated the difference in his life.

*

'Thank you for a delicious lunch. I don't know which I enjoyed more, the food or the conversation,' Lilliane chirped.

'I agree. My taste buds and my brain cells have both reported the highest levels of fulfilment.'

Kinetikus paid the bill and, when the waiter brought their coats, he shook his head and said: 'We won't need our coats until later.'

He took Lilliane by the hand, led her through a side door down a flight of narrow stairs through a hallway and into a darkened room.

Lilliane could see shiny red leather armchairs in rows and a well proportioned screen at the front.

'Is this a cinema?'

'Yes, and we will have it all to ourselves.'

'I did not know that hotels had cinemas.'

'Not all of them do, but a few of the central ones have private screening rooms for film directors, producers and press, to watch movies before they are released for general viewing. Some of them are available for private hire.'

'Are you saying you chose a movie for us to see now?

'Yes, I did.'

'She leaned back in one of the luxurious leather armchairs, and marvelled at the stylish layout of the room.'

'The seats are designed by a famous Italian car manufacturer.'

'I am not really into cars, but I love the seats,' she said with a very contented smile.

He looked at her, *I like her cute profile,* and made a sign to the projectionist to start the movie.

She loved every minute. *I feel very safe with him. It's so nice to sit next to each other, without feeling awkward in any way.*

He had picked a French movie with subtitles that had caught his interest in a review.

Lilliane was totally absorbed in the movie.

He caught the light dancing on her face.

"He is one of my favourite actors," she whispered to him.

It was an epic movie.

As the lights went back on, Kinetikus and Lilliane were in a daze.

'What a movie,' he sighed.

On their way out, the projectionist smiled at them.

'Did you like it?' he asked.

'It was wonderful,' Lilliane replied.

'Did you know there is a second feature length part to it?'

'What?'

'Yes, there is a continuation to the story in a second movie.'

Kinetikus looked at Lilliane.

'Do you have it here?' Kinetikus asked the projectionist.

'Yes, I think so.'

'Is the room free this evening?' Kinetikus asked.

'We have no further bookings until tomorrow night and, if you want, you can watch the second part in two hours.'

Lilliane looked at her watch. It was 4.30. The party begun at 8:30. She looked at Kinetikus who gave her a questioning look.

'Do you have plans for tonight?' he asked.

'Well, I have been invited to a party that I meant to attend. When would the movie finish?

'At about 8.30pm'.

Lilliane looked torn. 'I guess I could join the party a little later...what the heck, I really want to watch the second part. I need to know how it ends, now that I know that there is another part.'

Kinetikus smiled.

'I guess, that means I will see you in two hours,' said the projectionist and left the cinema.

Kinetikus and Lilliane sat down in the red leather armchairs.

'I did not know, that there was a second part to the movie when I picked it. How amazing! What shall we do now?'

'Let's have afternoon tea in the Brasserie and talk about the movie.'

'Sounds fine. I am sure they have got a beautiful selection of French Pâtisserie here.'

'I tend to prefer savoury food, but never say no to a crème brûlée and a fruity cup of tea.'

'What are we waiting for?'

The waiter smiled at them in recognition as they entered the Brasserie. Four cups of tea, one crème brûlée and a strawberry cheesecake later, they were still talking about the film.

'Did you realise that the movie was about exactly the same subject that we talked about over lunch? The hero was physically unattractive but was comfortable in his skin, and at the end, the girl falls in love with him.'

'Luckily, I don't have any physical distortions that could stop you from falling in love with me,' Kinetikus joked. 'AND I know who I am.'

'Yes, but you are not my type,' Lilliane assured him with a smile.

'I am relieved to hear that, and can confirm that you are not my type either, as I do not have a type.'

*

The second movie left a lasting impression on both of them. Lilliane had given up on trying to suppress her tears during the screening, as she noisily blew her nose with toilet paper. Kinetikus suddenly felt very protective towards her and offered her a soft tissue. She looked at him red eyed, and was surprised to see that Kinetikus also had tears in his eyes. After the movie, they stayed in silence for a while.

She got up. 'I have had an amazing time, and I don't feel like going to a mediocre party now. In fact, I am hungry.'

'I guess it's Brasserie time again.'

'I could get used to watching movies and dining all day long.'

'If you had not kissed strangers in a pub, we would not be here now,' he pointed out.

'A terrible experience led to the time of my life.'

'Mistakes are always blessings in disguise. We don't learn much from being right, it's our mistakes that harbour the gift of growth.'

Lilliane looked pensive. 'Let's reward ourselves for all our mistakes from now on.'

'I agree although it's equally important to celebrate our positive achievements. This is a lesson I learnt, a while ago, before I started my own company. I would set myself a goal at my work and, once I accomplished my target, I immediately focused on the next one. I felt stressed and did not enjoy my work. In fact, I was close to burnout at one stage.

'A friend helped me see that I was only ever looking at where I wanted to be, and never stopped to enjoy where I already was or look at what amazing journey lay behind me. He suggested that I make a list of all my achievements, big ones and little ones. Too often, we don't acknowledge the little results and positive changes in our life. I have developed my own ways to celebrate pretty much anything. I might say powerful encouraging words to myself, make a fun physical gesture, do a celebration dance to my favourite music or go on grand days out like today.' He laughed. 'I admit, I don't always celebrate like this. This was very special.'

He continued. 'I realised, that it's not the results that count but the way we feel about our results. At one stage, I felt terrible because I saw my results as a reminder of what I had not achieved yet. Now the same results remind me of how far I have come and I feel very happy. But it was my choice all along on how to react. My other mistake was to think that I did not deserve certain things, until I had become successful according to my own terms. When I started to question these terms, I realised that they were not really my own at all. I redefined success for myself and I am very happy with my work now. We think, to be happy, we need to do certain things, yet *being* is not related to *doing*. We can be happy for no reason at all. Have you tried that? Once you stop buying into the belief that you have to have a reason to be happy, you can experience how much fun you can have.'

Lilliane laughed. 'Yes, the happiest times in my life were the most spontaneous, unplanned situations, that were not related to any achievements in the normal sense. I always feel very happy and relaxed when I am in contact with nature. Sometimes I look at flowers and feel so grateful for their beauty. The other day, I came off the train and noticed two small flowers growing right on the railway track. It's quite a barren place and, in the past, I had only noticed strong grasses growing between the gravel on the tracks. I felt so much love and respect for these flowers. How can they survive with trains rushing over them every half an hour? They were so dainty and beautiful. I felt very encouraged by them and thought that, if they can live in the face of death and stand the heat day after day, I had really nothing to fear in my life.'

'Thank you for sharing that with me,' Kinetikus said softly.

'Thank you for reminding me, that I can be outrageously happy for no apparent reason at all.' She laughed and paused. 'But then do we need any reason to celebrate either? We can celebrate our mistakes, we can celebrate our little and big achievements, but we can also celebrate just for the sake of it. I love this.' She continued: 'I have got a great idea. Once a week let's do something to celebrate being alive and being able to celebrate.'

'I'm on!' *That's my kind of girl.*

Kinetikus was happy. On the way to work he had chosen to take a different route and walked via the train station. He had found some flowers on the railway track and taken a picture with his phone.

'Kinetikus, do you know anybody who might be interested in two opera tickets for tomorrow night?' his assistant asked from her desk. 'Ben and I have to cancel, because our daughter is in hospital expecting her first baby.'

'Not really. I have never been to the opera myself.'

'Why don't you try something new then?' she joked.

'You're right! How can I know what it's like, unless I try it myself. I'll take your tickets.'

Kinetikus found it a little challenging to focus on his work. He was eager to tell Lilliane about this week's celebration plans.

*

Lilliane had made her favourite tea, changed into her old pyjamas and dressing gown, and was lounging on her orange sofa. She was waiting. *He always calls me; maybe I should suggest that we share the costs.*

She was startled by the impatient ring of the phone. *He is early.*

'Hi!'

'Hi! I've got some news for you.'

'Fire away.'

'Have you had any thoughts about our celebrations for this week?'

'No, not really. Maybe I could cook something nice for us. A true celebration must involve food in some shape.'

He laughed. 'I really like the way you love food.' *She has got a great appetite for life.*

He had not thought about it but said quickly, 'Don't worry, I'll cook for us in my flat before we go out. I have got two tickets for the Opera for tomorrow night. We can walk there from my place.'

'Really? I love Musicals and the Opera. What do you like?'

'Actually, I have never been to the opera before but thought I might like to try something new with you. I came across the tickets by chance; my assistant sold them to me. She was unable to go with her husband.'

'You have never been to the Opera before? Well, I am sure you will like it. But it also depends quite a bit on what's on. What are we going to see?'

Kinetikus hesitated.

'I don't know.'

'What do you mean, you don't know? '

'I did not ask. I like surprises. I just got the tickets.'

'You bought tickets for an opera you know nothing about?'

'Yes, I am sure we will have fun whatever we do.'

He could feel her frustration.

'Generally, I like to know a little bit more about how I spent my valuable time and money,' she huffed.

'I paid for the tickets,' he reminded her gently."

'I don't understand how you did not even ask for the name of the opera.'

'I like to be surprised.'

'What if it is really boring and you then base your idea of operas on one terrible performance?'

'Let's not be afraid of something, that might or might not happen.'

She said apologetically, 'I guess, I like to make sure that we have a good time. I like a bit more…'

'Certainty?' he finished her sentence.

'Yes.'

'Did you know that the need for certainty is what holds most people back from being spontaneous. Everybody has a primary need for certainty or security. We all want to feel safe. Yet how would it feel if you had certainty about everything. Wouldn't it be terribly boring if we knew everything already? Experience has shown me that the more uncertainty I welcome into my life, the more enjoyable life becomes. Let's face it. We cannot plan for every second. Some things will always happen unexpectedly. If you feel bad every time something does not go according to plan, you have got one thing planned for sure; the feeling of constant failure. For example, I expected you to be happy that I had tickets for the opera but was a little surprised by your reaction. However, I did not feel angry with you. What is important, is how we respond to unexpected events. How flexible are we really?'

'I thought I was very flexible", she said quietly, 'but now I am not so sure. I am sorry for not truly appreciating the tickets.'

'It's no problem. I am on your side.'

'I have just understood something new about myself.'

She sounded excited.

'I definitely have a strong need for certainty but I believe my need for uncertainty is much higher. That's why I got myself into a lot of trouble in the past. I think, deep in my soul, I love uncertainty more than anything. Before leaving my partner my need for certainty held me back from truly changing anything. When I finally allowed complete uncertainty into my life and ended the relationship, I felt truly free. Since then I have been thriving on uncertainty, but the old need pops up always when I least expect it. Do we really need any certainty about anything at all?'

'You have to answer that question for yourself although your answer is likely to change over time.' He continued, 'What is most important is your awareness of it. Now that you have identified your need for certainty, you can consciously choose to change and welcome more uncertainty into your life. We cannot change something if we are not aware of what we wish to change.

'My grandmother once said to me "What we know is little. What we don't know is more. And what we don't know that we don't know is the most." It benefits us to welcome that there is always more to learn. It is important to stay open to new ideas or information,' he told her.

'I learn a lot when I talk to you,' she said.

'Believe me, I learn at least as much as you. I have to remind myself of these things, too."

"Maybe that's what a real friendship is all about. Learning from each other, and not being afraid to criticise each other. I am not usually very good at taking criticism but, I can feel, that you say something because you care and not because you want to hurt me.'

'I am glad to hear that.'

'Let's promise that we will be completely honest with each other, particularly, if we can help the other person see how they can grow.'

'Done!'

'I really look forward to tomorrow night.' she said.

"Me too!'

*

Lilliane found, that she was excited to see where he lived. She was curious. *I bet he has got a very stylish home. If I ever invite him to my flat, I will have to start tidying up three days beforehand.* She approached the three-story house. The neighbourhood was unfamiliar to her but she could tell that it was elegant, with tree lined avenues and lovely shops and cafes within walking distance of his home. *He lives in the top flat.* Lilliane rang the door bell of Flat no. 3. and heard Kinetikus' voice answering promptly through the intercom.

'Come in. The door is open. I am in the kitchen.'

51

She walked up the stairs and could smell a delicious mix of Mediterranean spices. The hallway was painted in a deep purple, and indeed the kitchen was a shining example of style, with stainless steal appliances and black marbled tops. *This is so different to my old kitchen.*
He was stirring a sauce and she could smell fish baking in the oven.
"Hi! I have just put in some new potatoes to cook. Please take a seat in the living room. Treat this like a restaurant. I will serve the starter in a minute.'
We are having a starter! Lilliane could feel her mouth begin to water. He seemed occupied, and she moved into the lounge where a big modern glass table was laid beautifully. She sat down and looked around with a sense of recognition. *I knew it would look like this.*
Jazz music was playing softly in the background, and she began to relax.
Kinetikus was carrying two plates with a mixed leaf salad and placed one in front of her.
'Milady, the prawn cocktail will follow shortly!'
He rushed back into the kitchen.
She smiled, leaned back in her chair, and listened to the music.
Kinetikus joined her carrying in two orange bowls.
'Here we are! Bon appetit!'
Lilliane watched as he began to eat. She felt a lump in her throat. He looked up. 'Are you alright? Don't you like fish?'
She lowered her gaze. 'I love fish and I love this, all of it. The music, the setting, the food. I can't remember the last time someone cooked for me. Thank you Kinetikus, I really appreciate this.'
He saw her eyes glistening with tears.
'Hey, it's so much more fun cooking for two. It's a pleasure."
I can't remember the last time I felt like cooking for anyone

either.

The meal was delicious.

'You were right about surprises,' Lilliane looked happier now. 'I think it's great that we don't know which opera we are visiting. It's exciting. Sometimes, if I have advance information about an event, I look forward to it so much that I begin to imagine the actors, the stage or whatever details of the event come to my mind. When things turn out to be different, as they inevitably do, sometimes I get a sense of disappointment. If I have no expectations, I don't set myself up for disappointment. I simply appreciate the moment.'

'Yes, the most unexpected moments often feel like presents to me too.'

'Are you ready for desert?' Kinetikus asked now.

'Absolutely.'

Kinetikus put a smooth crystal bowl in front of her.

'What is it?'

'Well, Miss Certainty, why don't you find out yourself?'

She tried a spoonful and her eyes widened in surprise.

It was Orange and Elderflower sorbet.

*

Kinetikus had changed into evening wear. During the performance he felt her gaze on him a couple of times. His soul rejoiced. She had begun to see him through the eyes of a woman.

*

During the break she insisted on buying him a glass of champagne from the bar.

An older lady complimented her on her orange dress.

'It's nice to see a change from black at these events. You look great in orange.'

'Thank you, Orange is my favourite colour.'

'Did you enjoy the first opera?'

'Do you mean the first half?'

'No. Did you not know they are showing two individual shorter operas by the same composer tonight? It's a special night. Both of them are shorter pieces that are not related to each other. Perfect, if you get bored easily with opera, like me.' She smiled.

Lilliane could not believe her ears. She could not wait to tell Kinetikus.

Her mind was buzzing. *This is the second time we have come to see one show, and were not aware that there is a second separate part to it. It truly is beautiful to be given something unexpectedly. Two individual parts forming one experience.*

She debated whether to tell Kinetikus as she did not want to spoil his surprise, but decided that it would confuse him more if she didn't.

He was amused when she told him.

'I did think that the first part had something like an end already and I was curious to see how it continued. I really enjoyed it. So we are getting two operas for the price of one. Just as we were shown two movies instead of one the other day.'

'It seems the universe wants to introduce the pleasures of opera in a mild manner to you.'

*

When the orchestra began to play the theme music of the second opera, Kinetikus and Lilliane looked at each other in a shock of recognition. It was the same piece of instrumental music that had played an important role throughout the French movies they had watched. The movies and the operas were related in more than one way. They were two totally different events chosen on random days, without knowing either of them. Lilliane was used to all sorts of strange and beautiful happenings but she realised that she had not previously experienced them with another person.

*

Kinetikus had loved the second opera. *If it had not been for Lilliane, I would never have seen this.*
'Would you like to talk about your virgin opera experience?'
He smiled. 'Great! Let's go back to my flat and chat over a cup of tea.'
They walked back. Lilliane was unusually silent and Kinetikus felt that she was fighting some kind of inner battle. When they arrived, she sat down in one of his armchairs with her arms crossed.
Have I said anything wrong?
'I have some strawberries in the fridge. Would you like some?' he asked.
Lilliane's posture opened a little.
'Yes please, that would be nice.'
He came back with a bowl of cut strawberries, and noticed that she had gone back into her closed state.
'Did you prepare them because you thought we would come back here afterwards?' she asked. Kinetikus sensed fear in her voice.
'Yes, I thought we might like to talk about the performance. I love strawberries and thought we might be peckish again after a couple of hours.'
She relaxed a little.
'Why are you afraid of love?' Kinetikus asked gently.
She stared at him. Her face displayed a mixture of shock, fear and anger.
'It doesn't last,' she replied slowly, without looking into his eyes.
'Maybe it didn't last in the past but does that mean that it can never last?'

55

'All my relationships started with great love, openness and friendship, but as soon as they became physical, they deteriorated. I think sex can harm a great friendship. I am very happy the way things are.'

Kinetikus looked pensive.

'For me, it is the other way round. Making love has always been the most fulfilling part of my relationships. Communicating through my body feels effortless. But the hurtful words that were in between never matched the connection that I felt during a physical union. I have never experienced total openness and great friendship in my relationships.'

'But you are open and I feel it's very easy to talk with you,' Lilliane said, 'I can't imagine, that you have problems communicating with anyone.

He hesitated, 'I find it easy with you. I don't find it as easy with everybody. In fact, I had become a bit of a recluse before I met you and I had come to prefer my own company. It's quite easy to do small talk but that's different. Some of the things we talked about I have never expressed before now. It's as if you draw them out of me. Sometimes I am amazed at what I say. I am learning about a different side of me, and I've never enjoyed talking so much. But even more than talking, I love listening to you.'

'It's the same with me. I am learning from you and never knew communicating can be as easy as this.' She laughed. 'And I am not exactly known for finding it hard to express myself in words. But…,' she stopped.

'But what?'

'I have found it more difficult to communicate with my body.'

'Have you always felt like this?'

'What do you mean?'

'Have you ever had a great intimate experience?'

She looked at him.

He could feel a wave of sadness and despair entering the room.

'Never,' she said.

An ocean of tears covered with gravel and cement.

He was surprised and asked, 'What about the very first time you made love? What happened?'

'We were very young when we met, and he came from a strictly Catholic background. We felt pressure to wait until I was at least eighteen years old. He was a lovely man and waited for over four years until I was nineteen. By that time we had become like brother and sister. My natural desire to make love to him had come and gone.'

'When you felt sexual energy for the first time, how did you express it?'

'I didn't really. I was deeply influenced by our local priest whom I admired. I went to a church school in the afternoons, and was taught religious education by this man. He was extremely old fashioned and I felt dirty when he told us that we had to confess whenever we touched ourselves. Up until then, I had not realised that it was considered a sin, and had enjoyed my body freely.'

Kinetikus looked at her. 'Do you think making love is dirty too?'

'No, I know in my mind that it is not, but it seems that my body doesn't feel that way. Whenever I felt any desire for a man, it only lasted until the moment we made love. I felt angry at myself for not feeling much during sex, and started to blame them.'

She looked lost. *She is so innocent.*

He needed to ask her this question:

'Do you **want** to feel?'

The cement is cracking.

'Yes,' she whispered. He sensed her tears.

'I want nothing more,' she cried.

There were ancient and long forgotten tears, angry and outraged tears and finally relieved and fresh tears.

All of them were pristine to him.

*

Kinetikus lay awake in his bed reflecting on the evening. Lilliane had taken a taxi home a while ago. They had talked as never before. She had remembered how a long time ago, before she began to censor her lust, she had felt truly alive and spontaneous in her body.

The hug she had given him to say goodbye was shorter than the others. Yet he knew, it was the first time she had felt his heart close to hers.

*

For a long time now Kinetikus had known, that they were meant to be lovers.

From the moment he saw her feminine beauty at his office, he desired her. Yet, whenever they had met, his mind was taken captive on a journey of boundless expansion and inspiration. He had grown addicted to her voice, addicted to her words. She had a language for the miracle of life, and planted countless seeds of new words within him. They had grown into strong flowers on a railway line. He knew that the time would come when she would run out of words to express her rising passion for life and love. A passion that can only be free in a realm beyond words.

*

Lilliane's fundraising party was in full swing. Kinetikus was listening to the band and observed Lilliane who was fluttering from guest to guest. *A sparkly orange butterfly.* He could tell from the tiny drops of sweat forming on her nose and cheeks, that her enjoyment was mixed with excitement and a little nervousness. She had just held the raffle and seemed unfamiliar with applause. Afterwards she rushed towards him and whispered in his ear, 'Could everybody hear me? I was a little nervous going onto the stage at first but, when I was up there I thought of the disabled girl and, suddenly realised that the raffle really had nothing to do with me at all. Everything seemed easy from that moment onwards.'

People were complementing her on the decoration of the hall. *Kinetikus and I spent the whole afternoon preparing the venue.*

All night he had the pleasure of looking at her. He knew that she was aware of his eyes upon her. *Don't be afraid Beautiful.*

*

The last guests left and Kinetikus and Lilliane found themselves alone in the hall. It looked quite a mess. She collapsed onto a chair. 'Oh dear, I did not realise how much hard work these events are! How could I be so naive to think I could do it on my own? If you had not helped me decorate and test the technical equipment and the lights today, it would have been a nightmare. I decided to do the party well before I met you. Boy, was I lucky to meet you when I did! I can't believe that I did not even think of asking anyone else to help me. Maybe I have an issue with asking for help. I always think I can do everything better on my own. I felt so good being responsible for myself for the first time in my life, but, I guess, it's impossible to do everything on one's own.'

She sighed and looked at the debris left to be cleared. Kinetikus understood.

'Come on! If we start immediately, we will be out of here in under two hours. I'll help you. We can do it.' He grabbed a broom.

'Stop! It's better to get everything off the walls first, and then deal with the floor, otherwise we'll have to sweep the floor twice,' she said.

'That makes sense! Let's put on some funky music and pretend we are partying for longer.' He picked out a disc.

She began to see the situation with slightly different eyes. George Benson was now blasting out of the stereo. "…What we have is much more than they can see…!" They smiled at each other and started to move to the music while clearing up the remains of the party.

He had been right. Exactly 110 minutes later, she locked the door to the hall and collapsed for the second time that evening as she got to her car seat.

'We made it! Thank you so much for all your help. I could not have done it without you.'

'I had fun.'

'Please stay at my place and get a good night's sleep, if you don't want to pay for a taxi home,' she offered.

'I have a guest bedroom,' she hastened to add, blushed, and hoped he would not notice.

He did.

'Sounds like a good idea to me, and I am very interested to see how you live.'

Lilliane suddenly had a look of terror on her face. *My place looks anything but presentable.*

'It's rather untidy so don't be shocked. I have not had much time recently to clean or tidy.'

'As long as I find a mattress somewhere to lay down my head, I'll be fine.'

She breathed a sigh of relief. 'Actually, the second bedroom is the tidiest room in the flat. I hardly use it, so you'll be fine.'

Kinetikus woke up to the sound of the birds. The sun was rising. His face caught the first rays through the curtainless window. It was still. *Lilliane must be asleep. I will have a shower and see if I can surprise her with breakfast.*

He threw on his clothes and took a brisk walk to the nearest corner shop, where he bought a toothbrush. On his way back, he passed a small supermarket and remembered that he did not know if Lilliane had any food to make breakfast. He bought strawberries, a mango, a pineapple and two Kiwis to make a fruit salad. Tempted by the smells of a bakery, he could not resist some freshly baked chocolate croissants and two small apple tarts. *I have no idea what she normally has for breakfast.*

Back in her flat, he went into the bathroom and smiled. The shower curtain and towels were orange. *Her essence is in here.*

He had a quick shower, found a white towel in the cupboard, and wrapped it around his waist. At that moment Lilliane walked in sleepily with one eye still closed, and was just preparing to sit down on her toilet, when she noticed him standing in the corner. He was watching her with a big smile on his face. She woke up instantly.

'Oooh, I did not know you were in here.' She looked embarrassed.

'How long have you been awake?' she asked.

'Not that long,' he replied. *Tangerine crinkled pyjamas.*

'Why don't you have a shower and I'll prepare some breakfast for us?' he continued.

She stared at him.

He was not sure if it was because he was only wearing a towel, or because she was surprised that he suggested to prepare breakfast.

'Hmm, I am not quite sure what we could have. I have got some organic muesli and apple juice. Not very exciting.'

'Don't worry, I am known to be a magician when it comes to food.'

She liked the sound of that.

'Good luck,' she said, 'I won't be very long.'

'Take your time.'

He found a large bowl in the kitchen, prepared the fruit salad and boiled some water for tea. The sun was flooding the lounge and Kinetikus looked around him with renewed curiosity. The large framed print above the fire place brought a smile to his face. The walls and wooden floorboards were painted off-white, and orange pieces of furniture and artwork were spread throughout the open plan room. He noticed a number of abstract oil paintings on canvas resting against the walls. *I think she mentioned that she paints.*

Numerous books were piled on the dark wooden dining table, old bookshelves and side tables. There were candles of all shapes and forms. He was amazed by the amount of different chairs in the room. One particular chair caught his attention. It looked hand-made, covered in a glossy fine skin with many folds. Electric blue glass in a bubble relief adorned the mostly black chair on the back rest and formed a vase shape.

'Are you admiring my underwater throne?' Lilliane said entering the room. 'I made that when I was studying for my A-level exams. After hours of reading I would go into our cellar to work on my chair and relax. Somebody once said it looks like a Gaudi piece. Anyway, I am curious to see what you found for breakfast.'

'It's on the table in the kitchen. Come through!'

She went quiet when she saw the brightly coloured fruit salad, croissants, tarts, muesli, tea and apple juice.

'I left the cave, went hunting for some deer, caught a huge one but let it go, and climbed a couple of trees instead to pick these.'

She laughed. 'Strawberries don't grow on trees!'

'That's why it took so long to find them.'

'I don't usually eat pastry for breakfast, but these croissants smell divine.'

She sat down with a very satisfied look on her face. 'You were right, you are a magician. This is the best breakfast I have seen for a long time. Thank you.'

'This is the first breakfast we share,' he commented.

She nodded and enjoyed eating.

He looked out into the garden.

'It's a beautiful sunny autumn day,' she said. 'I would love to go for a walk after breakfast. Are you free to join me, or do you have other plans for today? '

'No, nothing specific,' he replied. 'Usually I go jogging on Sundays or I catch up with the housework or shopping. Sometimes I meet friends or read and relax. Yes, I would love to join you for a walk after breakfast.' Lilliane suddenly knew, where she wanted to take him. She was debating, whether to tell him or wait to see if he would recognise his environment. Her decision was easy. *He loves surprises.*

The car pulled into a small parking lot facing a park. A few joggers looked as if they had been running for quite a while already. Lilliane led him across the park and through an iron gate into what looked like another park.

Kinetikus felt that the energy was different. Peaceful and calm. It was not long before he noticed gravestones in between the meadows and patches of neatly manicured lawns. They walked along a wide gravel path, which was lined with old oak trees.

'What amazing trees! This place feels quite special.'

Lilliane had been silent.

'It is very special to me,' she said. 'I have not been here for a long time. You are the first person I've brought here.'

He suddenly knew where they were, and looked at her.

She could see gratitude in his eyes.

'Close your eyes,' Kinetikus said softly. 'I will guide you. Don't speak and keep your eyes shut. Just trust me.'

Lilliane could feel his hand holding firmly onto her arm and gently pulling her forward. *What is he doing?*

She took a couple of clumsy steps forward, unused to walking without the sense of sight. He took her hands on a journey of discovery. A multitude of shapes, textures, temperatures and energies. She felt the patient, rough bark of older trees with their accepting, open lines and groves; her hands touched the cool, damp surface of freshly fallen leafs, soft grasses swaying gently in the wind, and smooth pebbles slowly adapting their shape to the flow of the icy water of a little stream. With each step she relaxed more deeply and, eventually, surrendered completely. She felt the fresh autumn breeze on her face, warm sunrays bathing her body in energy as her legs carried her hips effortlessly. Their steps synchronised. She learned to follow every minute movement of his arm and became an extension of his body. When he accelerated his steps, she burst out in exhilarated laughter. He was demanding the ultimate in trust of her.

I am running with closed eyes.

Her senses as acute as lightning, she ran straight into his arms.

Breathless and laughing hysterically, she wanted to fly forever.

*

Kinetikus picked up the phone at his office.

'I've missed your voice all day,' Lilliane said.

It was the first time that she called him in the afternoon, the first time she could not wait until the evening.

He had felt the same. After spending an entire weekend with Lilliane, he found it difficult to focus on anything else.

'I would like to take you to a classical concert tonight. One

of my tutors plays the piano and is giving a recital at a local church for free. I only just found out.' She sounded breathless. *Did she run to the phone?* 'What time does it start?' 'At seven. You could come over to my place by six thirty and we can go in my car.'
'What about now?'
'Don't you have to work?'
'I am the boss, I can take time off whenever I like.'
'How soon could you be here?'
I'll wrap up here, take a shower, change into casual clothes and hop straight into a taxi from home. I could be at yours in two hours at the latest.'
'Great! That should give me enough time to tidy up and cook something.'

*

The church was simple and uncluttered. They sat down on one of the front benches. Listening to the first note, they felt content and grateful, as the music bore the hidden gift of allowing their energy fields to merge. A reason to be close for a little eternity. Neither of them was very familiar with classical music but, through an innate understanding, they began to feel its beauty. A language without words, complex in its potential for expression, yet divinely simple at the same time. *What is the frequency of healing?*

*

Back in the car, words were few and far between. Lilliane's home baked German-style rye bread and hearty vegetable soup were delicious and the perfect antidote to a cold starry night announcing the winter. *May this food nurture my body, mind and soul and give me courage.*
Lilliane looked at the huge full moon outside.

'When I was little, I used to sleepwalk on nights of the full moon. One night my parents could not find me anywhere in the house and, eventually, saw me sitting in the middle of our garden, staring at the moon. I still find it hard to sleep on such nights.'

'I have always liked lunatics,' he said with a reassuring smile.

'I don't really feel like talking.'

Lilliane looked vulnerable and childlike without words.

She was unaware that she had long surrendered to his world.

Kinetikus felt a deep desire to protect her.

She looked into his eyes.

The gateway to his soul.

He is absolutely gorgeous. What a fool I have been!

Slowly she took his right hand, placed it into her left hand and truly looked at it for the first time.

'Yesterday these hands guided me. They are beautiful.'

She very slowly traced the life line of his hand with her index finger.

Further fingers joined in. They followed the horizontal lines and discovered the creases of his finger joints.

Joyously and innocently they floated over his hand as directed by her soft gaze, cupped his palm and playfully circled his fingertips.

A virgin landscape explored by a sensual adventurer.

Kinetikus felt her breath on his hand and closed his eyes.

These hands have touched a lot, yet they have never been truly touched. He was speechless.

She was leaving fingerprints on his soul.

*

Lilliane's soul retracted like a shy bird as his confident fingers began to respond to her touch with loving attention. They caressed every inch of her hand. Waves of energy were flooding her body with each new sensation. Every cell of her hand was alive.

Her fingers gently embraced his.

They interlocked loosely, only to part immediately.

Touched.

Separated.

Touched again.

Connected in a continuous light dance.

Their breathing synchronised.

It grew deeper and heavier.

His passionate fingers started squeezing and massaging her palm.

Lilliane closed her eyes. *Is it possible to make love with your hands?*

Her body was responding to his touch with overwhelming intensity.

She gasped for air.

'STOP! I can't breathe,' she laughed.

Kinetikus looked at her and leaned back in his seat with a contented smile.

'I have got a challenge for you,' he said.

'Go into your bedroom and enjoy your body! Continue the dance you began so beautifully. When you feel your energy build up ready to be expressed in its final release, repeat in your mind the words *I am free,* until the last wave of pleasure has subsided, and your breath has returned to normal.'

She looked at him in shock.

'You mean, now?'

'Don't hesitate. Ride with your arousal.'

'OK Mister but there is one condition.'

'Yes?'

'You do the same in the guest room.'

'Your command is my wish,' he joked.

'We just made love to each other,' he said waiting in the conservatory.

Lilliane had changed into her dressing gown. 'I guess, we could look at it that way,' she smiled a little self-consciously. 'I can't believe we just did that and you are sitting here so calm and composed, as if nothing has happened," she pretended to be outraged.

Kinetikus could tell that she was relaxed and very happy.

'Milady, I couldn't help notice a distinctive, healthy glow in your complexion. May I enquire as to the origin of this memorable sight?'

She laughed.

'I had my first double in six months of self-indulgence.'

'Fantastic, I can't quite compete with that, but enjoyed myself tremendously nevertheless.' They smiled.

Lilliane looked at Kinetikus. 'I feel, as if I've known you forever.'

'You probably have.'

'I dreamt of you, before I met you,' he said slowly. 'I heard an Orange Lily talk to me in German.'

'Do you think we were destined to be together?' Lilliane asked in a daze.

'I knew so, the night we met. I did not know if it was for romantic reasons or work related but strongly sensed that fate had brought us together. But, of course, according to you, we have created this reality ourselves.

'It looks as if our souls have been plotting all along.' He laughed and continued: 'I knew, we were supposed to be more than friends, when I first noticed you as a woman.'

'When?'

'At my office party.'

'What?'

'The moment I desired you, I knew that we were to become lovers.

In the nature of desire lies the seed for its fulfilment.
'As a young boy I would often see beautiful things and feel encouraged by them. I have always liked luxury cars, and understood that the universe would not show them to me, unless I was going to experience owning one myself. Other people choose to feel discouraged by the same things. What we focus on expands. If our thoughts are full of fears we attract the manifestation of our fears. If we focus on love and courage, we draw good things into our life.'
'I could not agree more. But, I am confused as to when I focused on attracting you into my life. As far as I remember, I was not looking for love at the time I met you. If anything, I was in love with myself and did not need anybody else in my life.'
'I was not actively looking either. However, I had been harbouring, for a while, a deep wish to meet someone. I felt full and happy in the knowledge that she could enter my life at any moment. Maybe this is the key. Neither of us was desperate for love. We had found it within ourselves. Only two whole people can create a union that is bigger than the sum of its parts.'
Kinetikus suddenly remembered something and smiled.
"I have to make a confession. Although I was not consciously searching for love when I met you, I feel certain that I designed you at a previous stage.'
Lilliane looked puzzled. 'What do you mean?'
'A while ago, I wrote down my intentions for my ideal woman in my notebook.'
Lilliane looked pensive.
Kinetikus continued, 'I have always felt that the written word has power over the spoken word and thoughts, which are creative tools in their own right. I write down everything that is important to me - my goals, insights and learning experiences. I keep one notebook especially for creative

ideas of any kind.'

Lilliane suddenly laughed out loudly.

He looked surprised.

'Yes, I also made a list a while ago. But I did not have any idea then how powerful this stuff can be.' She sighed.

'A little while after my experience at the cemetery, I made a list of attributes for a divine lover. I wrote out a few pages describing my ideal man.'

'Do you still have this list?'

'Yes.' Lilliane went to the chest of drawers, started rummaging through papers, and picked up a thin orange folder.

'Can I see it?' Kinetikus was intrigued.

'I am not sure. Let me have a look at it first." She began to read.

Lilliane smiled and laughed out loud a couple of times. She handed him the folder.

'You are astonishingly close already.'

He read:

I don't need anybody, especially not a man.
I am in love with myself.

If I ever fall in love again, it will be with someone so perfect for me that I'll love him more every single day of my life. He will let me overflow with love, so that I can share it with the world.
I will never ever settle for anything less.

He is very handsome in my eyes.
Has razor sharp intelligence, and no need to prove his intellect.
With a strong sense of self, he is totally independent from me.

He entertains me, makes me laugh and brings out my inner child.
We play together and forget ourselves.
He is kind and gentle in nature, yet a warrior at heart.
Sensitive to his environment, he respects the needs of others without compromising his own.
He is driven by his desire and openness to grow beyond himself.
He inspires me and is my teacher.
I inspire him and am his teacher.

The list continued for another two pages and Kinetikus thought with admiration that it was much more sophisticated and detailed than his.

He continued to read.

He admires and respects the wonders of nature. He feels connected to the universe.
He is awake, alive and in love with himself and life.

Kinetikus laughed when he read:

He does his own ironing and is no stranger to cleaning.
He displays an almost pathologic aversion to football and television.
He likes to cook, and nurture me in creative playful ways.

My deepest wish

He admires, respects and looks after his body with loving care.
He is my sensual superhero, who holds the key to unlock my true feminine essence.

I trust and surrender to his divine touch, and I am consumed by desire to merge with his body.
Together we discover unknown sensual heights, true intimacy and ecstatic bliss.
He sees the goddess in me, and worships my feminine beauty and creative power.
In endless gratitude we never grow tired of our minds, bodies and souls!!
We grow together and set each other free!

Kinetikus had tears in his eyes. He put the folder down.

*

Lilliane was sitting on her bed and wrote in her diary.
I am afraid of losing him, if we make love. But more than afraid, I am alive. We have chosen to discover our bodies like virgins. I have never experienced the flow of energy in my body like this before. It is as if he wakes up every fibre of my being with the touch of a single cell. Yesterday he touched my hair, and I could feel the vibration travelling down my neck, into my back, and collecting in rays in my female centre.
My hands surprise me in their playfulness and curiosity. I have become a child, who is discovering the world through touch. Blessed are our hands.

*

Kinetikus called Lilliane from abroad. *Sadly, I don't need a German interpreter in this country.*
'There is a distinctive lack of orange in this country,' he sighed.
She smiled.
'However, everything somehow reminds me of you.
We made love again last night,' he said softly.

'I was not with you.'

'You are always with me even when we are not together.'

'When did you...do something?'

'Last night after the conference, around midnight.'

'That's amazing, I woke up around that time and thought of you too.'

'How did you think of me?' he pressed.

'In the same way as you,' she teased.

'Tell me more about it.'

'Hmmm, I was worshipped and discovered, before I was conquered and ravished.'

Kinetikus smiled.

'I will make love to you in a hundred different ways before you beg me to make love to you in the way that only a man and a woman can. By then you will no longer be afraid.'

Lilliane swallowed, her heart beat faster.

'Am I in the hands of a master?'

'Yes, you are your own master.'

*

'I want to read you something.' Lilliane sat down cross-legged on her orange sofa. Kinetikus was joining her with two cups of herbal tea.

She sounded excited.

'Today, I found a poem that I wrote when I was 14 years old. I have never shown it to anybody. I feel that it was written for you all along.

Passion

Insignificant and mortal still,
the gentle force is floating down to the earth.
Aware of its warm power,
it bends down slowly and grabs me.

Colourful thoughts are sprouting in my subconscious mind:
pale red hills replace grey asphalt,
silent melodies are everywhere and here
My sensitivity knows no limits.

The stormy flower continues to grow in my heart.
Its immortal force is causing me pain.
Yet my willpower is unable to hold it back any longer.
It breaks free in a shivering hot flood of the senses.

Kinetikus was silent.

She began to wonder if he liked her poem, when he replied:

'I could feel it in my body.'

Lilliane was relieved, and moved into her usual talkative mode:

'I remember feeling so deeply, at the time, that I needed to write it down. Only a limited number of words felt right to express it.'

He seemed to process her comment for longer than expected.

She grew impatient and asked him, 'Did you feel it needed more words? '

He smiled and said slowly, 'No, it did not need more words! You said, that when you wrote it, you really felt it, and that is conveyed perfectly in your poem. Often when you talk about your emotions, you express them beautifully in colourful and descriptive words. The stream of words sometimes hardly allows you to breathe. I am wondering, how much do you actually *feel* when you talk?'

Lilliane went silent.

Kinetikus sensed that his question had gone deep to her core.

'Are you alright?'

Her voice was tear-laden.

'No, not really. I am confused. I think you might have a

point. I have never really thought about it. It is possible that…
'It's OK Beautiful, just let it all out.'
She began to cry.
'I think, that I often talk instead of allowing myself to feel.'
A wave of pain and realisation flooded her.
She collapsed in his arms.
'I…I have been in my fucking head for all this time.
No wonder, I couldn't feel much in my body.'
"I always carry a spare guillotine with me, just in case," Kinetikus commented.
She laughed through her tears.
Kinetikus looked at her, taking in her beauty.
I will always worship you.
He felt the energy building between them.
Lilliane slowly placed her hands over his face without touching it. He could feel the heat of her palms and closed his eyes.
Her hands were now gently resting on his eyes.
Lilliane felt the outline of his face with her palms.
His forehead, eyes, beautiful cheek bones and smiling cheeks. Her fingers brushed against his full lips before feeling his jaw line and masculine chin.
He took both of her hands into his and gently blew on them.
Lilliane felt a shiver down her spine.
He pressed his lips softly on the inside of her hands, discovering them afresh.
Breathless, she imagined how they would feel against her lips.

*

Lilliane had been awaiting the weekend impatiently. She called Kinetikus at seven in the morning, an unusually early hour for her. He had given her the nick-name Lazarussa, as

75

she would normally rise no earlier than nine; she could be very grumpy, if anyone disturbed her sleep before that hour.

'Let's drive down to the coast today, I love the sea. It looks like it's going to be a sunny day. I know it's autumn, and we'll need to wrap up warm but I like to feel the wind in my hair and smell the fresh salty breeze.'

Lilliane's words evoked a clear picture in his mind.

'What a great idea, let's get out of the smelly city. When should I come over?'

'I would like to prepare a picnic for us, and I hate being rushed. I also have not had a shower yet. Maybe around ten. It will take us about two hours to drive to a nice spot. We can go in my car, you know how much I love to drive and explore the countryside. Anyway, my car is bigger than your two-seater. It's much more practical,' she teased.

'No comment.'

*

Three hours later, she was just loading the car when Kinetikus arrived. He laughed when he looked into the car boot. It was full of equipment; a huge food hamper, folding chairs, blankets, pillows, a torch, books, CDs, drawing paper, crayons, and even a plastic toy bucket and spade for building sandcastles.

I understand why she did not want to go in my car.

'I love being on the move,' Lilliane exclaimed happily. 'Cars, trains, buses, planes, boats - anything that moves. Preferably fast!'

Driving onto the motorway, she turned the music up and began to sing loudly. Kinetikus joined in. After a while, he realised that he felt totally free to sing. It did not matter if he knew the song or not.

"You have got an amazing voice," Lilliane said and stopped singing. 'Mellow and soulful.'

'Thank you. You are a much more appreciative, and an infinitely more attractive audience, than my shower curtain.'
Lilliane imagined his shower curtain applauding and giggled.
Sunny autumn trees flew by.
The shadows of the clouds were dancing in the spotlight.
A magnificent silent movie proudly played on a panoramic windscreen, indifferent to approval, and eternally aware that no man could ever compete with its natural spectacle of light.

*

The sea was turbulent and, although the atmosphere had stored all that the early sun had to offer, the breeze gave away the season with brutal honesty. Wrapped up in their winter coats, armed with gloves and scarves, two unlikely heroes carried a multitude of items to a nearby beach. Apart from a few people walking their dogs in the distance, the beach was deserted.
Lilliane put a thick blanket on the ground.
'This is my special thermal picnic blanket. It is soft and cuddly on top, and has a waterproof insulated layer underneath.'
Kinetikus was impressed.
'I love gadgets,' he said with a smile. 'But you seem to beat my collection of useful things.'
'Actually, it was a present from my mum. She is the queen of common sense and practicality.'
'I always knew you were a princess.'
She did a courtesy, passed her prince the thermos jug with piping hot tea, and proudly began to spread out their feast.
Kinetikus felt very touched by the loving attention she had obviously put into preparing an array of hearty salads with sweet potatoes, lentils, colourful mixed vegetables and fresh greens.
They were both hungry. Breakfast had consisted only of fruit

juice.

'I am surprised that you lasted out until now,' Kinetikus teased. 'Normally, you need to eat something around eleven. I can set my watch by your hunger patterns.'

'You would make a great homeopath,' she laughed. 'Nothing escapes you.'

They finished their meal. Full and satisfied, they lay back on the blanket and looked up to the sky.

'Can you see that *heart* shape in the clouds?' Lilliane screeched.

'That's incredible! Nobody would believe us if we said that we saw a heart in the sky,' she lamented. 'It's so unreal.'

"Who cares? It's beautiful, and meant for our eyes only. I feel very grateful.'

'So do I,' she said humbly.

He took her hand, and they lay silently staring at the clouds.

After a while Lilliane grew restless, jumped up and ran off.

'Catch me, if you can.'

Kinetikus waited a couple of seconds, before responding to her challenge. *I'll give her a head start. My long legs will catch up with her in no time.*

Lilliane was shouting from a distance. The sound of the sea muffled her laughter. She ran as fast as she could. *It's harder than I thought to run on sand.*

She turned around.

Where is he?

Suddenly, two hands were covering her eyes from behind.

She screamed out in shock and heard a familiar laugh.

'How did you *do* that?'

'Well, while you ran off like a madwoman and only looked down at the sand in front of your feet, I ran down closer towards the sea, where the sand it wet and hard. It's much easier to run on it, and I caught up with you easily. By the time you turned around, I was already ahead of you.'

78

'You scared me,' she gasped, trembling a little.

He took her in his arms.

I can stay like this forever.

He gently took her face between his hands, and bent down towards her. Lilliane closed her eyes and felt his lips softly kissing her nose, her cheeks, and then her eyes. She anticipated feeling them on her mouth, and was surprised, to sense their soft impact on her neck. A wave of pleasure travelled down her body. His fingers were tracing the outline of her lips, while he continued to discover her neck with his mouth. She opened her lips slightly, willing to grant entry. They were teased to despair, and responded in reflex. Hungry to kiss, her mouth enveloped one of his fingers. Energy was flooding the centre of his body, as he felt her tongue circling around his finger. She pressed closer against his body, and became aware of the physical effect of her presence.

Lilliane smiled and was taken by surprise when his lips deliberately brushed against hers. Like his fingers, they knew how to lure her.

Please kiss me, I can't bear it any longer.

She pushed her lips against his. As their mouths opened, she felt her female mouth open, whilst two tongues tentatively joined on a joyful journey.

He gently lowered her down onto the cool soft sand.

The thermal blanket was nowhere in sight.

She did not care.

Time ceased to exist, the wind turned silent, and the sea softly serenaded their first kiss. For what seemed an eternity, the universe witnessed in awe the passionate encounter of two mouths.

Lilliane did not know where her mouth began and his ended. She felt his hands stroking her hair. Her body was flowing in a riot of sensations.

I am so alive, I want to scream.

She tore herself away.

'YES…YES…' Lilliane screamed into the wild wind.

'Let's do a cartwheel competition,' she shouted.

Kinetikus looked stunned.

Before he could reply, he saw her limbs flying in continuous wide circles, and watched in amazement as she completed seven cartwheels.

She had collapsed onto the sand.

He joined her. 'Wow, I've never seen anybody do that.'

'I don't even know, if I can do *one*. It's been quite a while.' She laughed. 'Go on then, try.'

Lilliane was in fits of victorious laughter, as she observed his futile attempts. *He is so adorable.*

The third one resembled a crooked version of a cartwheel, and she exploded in applause.

He bowed to the sea, to the sand and to his kind audience.

'I am hungry, let's have dessert. I have a surprise for you,' she laughed.

His eyes widened.

They raced back to the comfort of the thermal blanket. It had become their home.

Lilliane opened a big round container.

Apple pie, my favourite. Kinetikus was in heaven.

With an excited look on her face, she reached for a second smaller thermos flask.

'I hope it's still hot. I have never tried it with custard. I thought, if it can keep tea hot, why not custard.' *This woman is crazy, and I love it.*

The custard was perfect.

Lilliane enjoyed nothing more than watching him being happy.

I don't even like custard.

Despite all their efforts, they could feel the cold creeping up on them. The sun was preparing to set and the sky turning a distinctively darker hue.

By the time they had packed up and were ready to load the car, it was completely dark. Lilliane was happy to make use of another gadget. A head torch.

A silent procession of two slow shadows, this time with a slightly lighter load, followed a circle of light leading the way.

Back in the car, Lilliane turned up the heating and sighed.

'I've had a fabulous time today.'

'Me too. Thank you for the exquisite picnic. But the day has not ended yet,' Kinetikus pointed out. 'Let's go back to your place. There is enough food left to have another picnic.'

'What a lovely repertoire we have – talking, joking, singing, touching, kissing, eating, learning, watching moves and operas! How can people possibly be bored? I don't understand. 'Lilliane was happy.

'Don't forget, the list is always growing,' Kinetikus said with a sensual smile. 'This is only the beginning.'

'I feel so rich already, I wouldn't know where to put any new experiences.'

'You could always dejunk the ones you don't need anymore,' he teased.

'How?' Lilliane had turned more serious.

'Any thought that is painful, ultimately does not serve you. Whether it is a past memory you are dwelling on or a current issue, you can simply check in with yourself, how you feel while you think it, and decide if you wish to think it at all. You can always replace it with a more pleasant thought. It's your choice.'

Kinetikus' attention left the conversation for a moment, as he noticed a luxury car overtaking them on the motorway.

'That is one of my favourites. A beautifully engineered car, combining everything a car should have.'

'Well, fancy cars are obviously much more important than our conversation,' she said frustrated by his change of focus.

'Why are you angry? I only wanted to point it out to you, as it was passing by. I thought, you might be interested in finding out about things that I like.'

'I don't like people who show off their expensive cars, and I don't understand why you admire such ostentation. It's ridiculous to waste so much money on something, just because it looks nice.'

'If you want to know why I like beautiful cars, please ask me, instead of getting angry at some innocent people? The answer is, that I simply like nice things. I like good quality clothes, cars, furniture etc. It does not matter to me if anybody knows or can see how much money I spend. You have to ask yourself, why you think it's ridiculous to spend a lot of money on something, just because it looks nice. Why shouldn't you be able to? It should be your choice on what you do with your own money. It looks to me as if there are much deeper issues and prejudices at work here. If you had a million pounds, would you buy yourself a nice car?'

'Probably not,' she said. 'I'd buy a bigger house and invest some money. The rest I would use to help my family and help other good causes.'

'OK, that is very laudable. However, ask yourself why you feel that you have to give the rest of it away?'

'I don't think it's right to spend unnecessary amounts on myself?'

'Why?'

'I would feel guilty.'

'Bingo! Guilt! This seems to be a theme of yours. You feel guilty about lust. You feel guilty about money. If you don't know how to give to yourself, how can you possibly give to others. You would naturally begin to resent them, for taking that which you also desire. I think, your anger towards people living in luxury stems from a good dash of envy.'

'I don't know anybody, who is very rich *and* happy,' she protested steering the conversation away from herself.

'Well, many of the people I know and admire are very wealthy, happy and generous. This is a perfect example of what I was referring to earlier on. You seem to have a multitude of limiting beliefs about money which you could choose to examine closer, and de-junk the elements that don't serve you. Beliefs are much more powerful than individual thoughts because they are already established in our subconscious mind as, what we perceive to be the truth. We have stopped questioning them. Yet all beliefs are based solely on our interpretation of past experiences. Nothing is absolute. The same experience might mean something completely different to another person.'

'But how do I know, which beliefs serve me, and which don't?'

'Very easily. Limiting or disempowering beliefs make you feel miserable. They deplete your energy and passion for life. They come at a high cost. People who believe life is not fair, and that they never get what they want, will subconsciously attract events into their lives which will justify non-supportive beliefs. Negative thoughts, and especially beliefs, not only make us feel depressed, hopeless and powerless but, more importantly, have direct implications on our physical health. A study, at an American University, examined the saliva of a number of people during different patterns of thinking. Negative thinking patterns, which created emotions of anger, despair, jealousy etc. produced a measurable quantity of poison in the saliva, that was sufficient to kill rats. When we get angry, it is effectively the same as swallowing poison, but expecting somebody else to die.'

'Yes, I heard, that scientists have established a direct link between suppressed anger and developing cancer. When we treat a cancer with homeopathy, we also look at the emotions that have been suppressed over a long period of time.' She looked at him. 'How do you know all this stuff?'

'I love to read, and am fascinated with the human mind and its power to generate wealth.'

'I focus on health, and you focus on wealth. It sounds to me as if we are coming across similar principles. It's all the same thing really - clearing blockages and allowing the natural flow of energy. So how can I change my beliefs?'

'You establish a belief by collecting references for it. You can change a belief by consciously focusing on finding more references for a new empowering belief. For example, many people have early childhood references of money causing arguments between parents, of never having enough of it, or, of too much money causing pain of some sort. They have subconsciously adopted beliefs about money, according to what they have been told by others and experienced when they were young. We have all heard sayings like *Money is the root of all evil, Money is dirty etc.* In your case, you have a belief that money and happiness exclude each other. Now, one doesn't need to be a rocket scientist to understand, that with a belief like that, you would not attract financial freedom into your life. If you fear, that by becoming rich, you sacrifice your happiness, your subconscious mind will do anything to steer you away from wealth. If you honestly looked at the six different key areas of your life: love and relationships, emotional health, physical health, wealth, spirituality and contribution, and rated them on a scale of 1-10, according to how close to their ideal potential you are, how much would your wealth sector score?'

Lilliane witnessed her ego rise in protest, but decided to answer truthfully.

'Maybe four at the highest.'

'How does that compare to all other areas?'

'It's the lowest of them all.'

'Great, that's what I call a result. Now that you have become aware of it, you can focus on improving it. You could chose to find references for a new belief, that money is fun, e.g. think of all the fabulous activities you can do with some spare cash, like buying as many books as you like and going on adventure holidays for example. Keep focusing on this new belief. Imagine how it would feel like to spend money on anything you like.'

Kinetikus hesitated, but continued. 'One of the deepest issues that is holding people back from attracting abundance into their lives is the subconscious belief that they are unworthy of it. I addressed this issue with myself, when I became aware of it a while ago. Everybody deserves to be financially free.'

She turned silent and looked a little lost. Kinetikus wondered, if she was uncovering an old memory.

'What do you feel right now?' he asked.

'I feel sad and a little angry but I don't really know why. It was such a perfect day and now it's gone all...'

'All what?'

'All heavy...I was so unreasonable and judgemental about the car, and you became so grown up. And everything else you said also reminded me, that...'

She looked tearful, and Kinetikus wondered if it was safe for her to continue to drive.

'After my experience in the park everything felt so easy. I thought that I knew the answer to every question in the universe but, I guess, I am nowhere near as enlightened as I thought I was.'

'Hey, we are all human. I need to focus on my health more, for example, and I learn a lot from you. I think you are amazing. But we all tend to beat ourselves up about our mistakes. Remember, we chose to celebrate, every time we learn something?'

'I like the celebration part, but I am not so keen on the making mistakes part,' Lilliane admitted.

I want to squeeze and tickle her.

She parked the car outside her flat, Kinetikus unloaded the car while she rushed to the loo.

'I am still quite cold and have got sand in my hair.' She looked at him with a smile, remembering their time on the beach. 'I might have a hot shower.'

'Let me run you a nice hot bath, you've been driving a lot today. I'll call you when it's ready.'

Kinetikus disappeared into the bathroom, and she could hear the water filling the bathtub. She sat down on the sofa and wrapped herself in a blanket.

The bath was ready and Lilliane felt very touched when she saw her bathroom. The lights were off and Kinetikus had lit three of her favourite candles, transforming her bathroom into a sanctuary. She could smell her lemon bath gel as she took one sock off and dipped her big toe into the playful amount of foam. Lilliane kissed him gently on his cheek.

'Thank you. You are my hero. Now, get out of here!'

She closed the door and undressed.

The bath was glorious, and Lilliane lay still with her eyes closed for about fifteen minutes.

Kinetikus knocked at the door.

'Can I come in?'

'I am still in the bath.'

'I don't mind .'

Lilliane's heart began to beat. She looked down at the water in front of her. The foam covered her body completely.

'As long as you behave yourself and don't touch the water, you can come in,' she shouted.

'Hmm, I'll do my best.'

Kinetikus walked in with a bowl. It was full of grapes.
'I found these in your fridge, and wanted to feed you. It's indulgent.'
'Really? That's amazing,' Lilliane looked very pleased. 'I have a confession to make, I often eat ice lollies in the bath. I just love the contrast of the cold in my mouth and the hot water around my body. I guess we are two outlaws violating the common purpose of a bath.'
'The purpose of a bath is, what we make it,' said Kinetikus and popped a grape into her mouth.
She smiled. 'This is a worthy celebration bath.'
Lilliane could feel his eyes monitoring the movements of the foam.
'You do, of course, realise that I have a pretty good idea about your body shape already,' he teased. 'It's impossible to overlook the fact that you are a woman.'
'What do you mean?' she protested playfully.
'I have got an eye for female body shapes. It used to be something like a hobby. Believe me, you are absolutely perfect for me.'
'We'll see.'
'I can't wait.'
He was touching her with his eyes.
Kinetikus playfully blew on the bath foam in what seemed like strategic places. The foam was wearing thin, and Lilliane waited with baited breath.
Two small spy holes in the water exposed her nipples.
Sirens in the sea.

*

Lilliane's diary appreciated her attention.

When I am with him, I do not think about my actions. They just happen. My inner judge retreats to a place of care and

87

respect, as if this is my time off. I discovered, that I can let go of any concept of what is right or wrong, not only when I am in my private world but also with another person. I felt very aroused after my bath yesterday, and, to my surprise, suggested to Kinetikus that we pleasure ourselves together. My initial shyness wore off quickly with the realisation that he was completely comfortable with this level of exposure. Although we could not see or even feel our bodies underneath my blanket, we instinctively looked at each other at the crucial moment. I felt a deep connection with him and, a childlike joy at the insight, that I had found a true playmate.

*

It feels effortless to be in my body in his presence. I had no idea how little time I had spent in it. I mourned my lost time in his arms. Sweet tears cried in freedom. At times, I am overcome with gratitude, that it is possible to feel so alive, and to know that this is just the beginning.

*

I am in love with his hands. They are so gentle and perceptive, joyful and respectful. Like beings of higher intelligence, at times they know how and where to touch me, before I know myself. I feel his pleasure in caressing me, and am free to receive completely, without the need to give in return.
I am thirsty to receive all he wishes to give.

*

The impossible dream came true last night. I am free. I spent my first night at his flat, and completely surrendered to his touch. His hands made love to me in a way that I could never even attempt myself. At one point, my old inner saboteur made a vain attempt to diffuse the energy of pure pleasure that had built up in my body. I witnessed myself thinking: "You have never been fulfilled by a man's touch before, don't even consider it possible." The next voice was more quiet, and replied gently: "I agree completely, and am just going to enjoy whatever happens. "I did not know, that in this total acceptance lay the key to my bliss, and was taken by surprise, when my body lovingly overtook my mind only a few seconds after my surrender. Kinetikus had known the secret all along and witnessed the moment that my mind gave up on fulfilment with compassion. It did not intimidate him; he was forever present in his own joy and expression of continuous love. It was the energy of this love that was powerfully set free in shocked moans of delight, followed by tears of rage, relief and joy. I don't remember when I stopped crying, but I remember when I first saw his smile.

*

The next weekend had come, and Lilliane was redecorating her bedroom walls. She had decided to paint the back wall a deep purple. It would create a striking contrast against her orange bed. Kinetikus had offered to lend a helping hand. With precision he placed the masking tape around the edges of the skirting board, sticking it to the clear plastic sheet that was protecting the floor. Lilliane watched him, sighed and rushed into the kitchen.

'I can't watch you. I'll make some tea. Thanks so much for doing this for me. I am far too impatient. What's the problem with a couple of splashes of paint on the floor. It's water soluble, I can easily wash it off later.'

He smiled. 'I have come to love our differences. Particularly, the very obvious ones.'

He started painting the corners with a smaller brush, whereas she had begun in the middle of her side with a big paint laden roller. They looked at each other and laughed.

'I guess, it makes more sense to do it your way,' she admitted.

'Can you do all the corners, and I go wild in the middle?'

'You can go wild wherever you like, it is not limited to the wall of your bedroom,' Kinetikus replied.

'That reminds me, I won't be able to sleep in my bedroom tonight.' Lilliane was having a creative moment, and Kinetikus saw a flash of excitement glimmering in her eyes. He was hoping, that she would commit to spending another night at his flat.

'Have you ever slept in a tent before?' Lilliane asked.

His heart sank.

'No, I never really got around to it, and now prefer hotels, to be honest.'

'I love challenging you to new experiences.'

'Lilliane, it's very cold. The trees have lost all their leaves. You won't get me out of this place into a freezing tent.'

'Who said anything about going outside? We will put up a tent in my lounge. It will be so romantic.' She was running an imaginary scene in her mind, and smiled inwardly.

'I have a small double futon mattress and a big pop-up beach tent, that we can use. I even have a CD with soothing whale sounds, and we can pretend that we are near the seaside.'

Kinetikus was suppressing his laughter. *I have never heard whale sounds on the beach.*

'I like the idea of a small double futon mattress.' Kinetikus smirked at her.

Lilliane's attention went back to the wall. It seemed she was even more eager to finish it now. Her mind was already on her next project of building a love nest, and initiating Kinetikus to the pleasures of indoor camping.

Kinetikus was clearing the bedroom and cleaning the paint brushes. It had gone dark outside.

'You can come into the lounge now,' Lilliane shouted.
Kinetikus eyes had to get used to the darkness of the room.
The first thing he noticed, was a big bowl of flickering
floating candles in the middle of the room. In the
background, he made out the outline of a rounded tent.
'Imagine this is our campfire,' Lilliane's eyes sparkled.
'You are the maddest woman in the world. I feel like a
teenager with you.'
'It's the first time I've done this. You seem to bring out so
many fun ideas in me. I feel, you won't judge me, however
silly something might seem. Anyway, at least I am very
sensible when it comes to nourishment. I made some toasted
tuna sandwiches with tomato salad for us, nothing fancy.'
'Sounds fabulous.'
They sat down on two large orange floor pillows and ate. The
candlelight lit their faces.
Lilliane suddenly looked at Kinetikus with a childlike
expression.
She went to her cupboard.
'Pink marshmallows?' Kinetikus looked surprised.
'Where did you get these from now?'
'They were a present from a little girl at the clinic.
Homeopathy helped clear her eczema, and she gave me these
as a thank you. They have been in my cupboard for a while.
Do you think it's possible, to toast them over candles?'
'I am a total novice on toasting marshmallows, and would
advice to have some water nearby, in case anything goes out
of hand.'
Lilliane laughed.
'I don't really like sweets but I want to try this.'
She took a metal skewer, placed a marshmallow at the end of
it, and held it above the candles.
'It's working. Would you like to try? 'Lilliane was delighted.
She fed Kinetikus with the malleable, sugary mass.

'Yummy, tastes of vanilla.'

He prepared one for her.

'Hmm, quite nice, but I don't understand, how people can have more than one or two of these.'

Kinetikus had three more, and needed to follow up with a big glass of water.

He noticed a strange expression on her face.

'One of my first experiences with camping was with a Catholic youth group. I must have been about 10 years old. Of course, most of us girls had an innocent crush on the young priest who was leading the camp. I remember him reading a fairytale from a book to us. He had read stories from it before, and some of them were quite spooky, by the campfire. One night, he began to read a story of a huntsman, who fell in love with a beautiful woman. She lived near a lake on her own. There were rumours that she was dangerous but he did not believe them. One day, they were rowing on a boat in the middle of the lake. He could see beneath her skirt, and noticed, that she was not wearing any underwear. The priest, who was reading the story to us, suddenly looked stunned, turned red, and silently read a little further. He stopped reading and said, that he was going to read a different story for us on that night. But, of course, we were all extremely curious about the rest of the story. The next day, four of us got together and stole the story book from his tent. We hid in the forest and read the end of the story. It was the weirdest fairytale I have ever come across. The woman had teeth in her vagina. She was some kind of man eating monster. The man had noticed her teeth, but was so enraptured by her beauty that he was prepared to die. They made passionate love and somehow the teeth did not harm him. She cried and confessed that she had killed many men in the past, as her teeth had never stayed open, but caused many a bloodbath in the moment of passion. He had ended her spell by his willingness to die for her. All the men before him had been afraid of death. After we finished reading the story, one of the girls suggested that we check if we had any teeth in our vaginas. We all examined each other. I remember thinking that I liked being touched, but more than enjoying the sensation, I was very relieved to find out, that I had absolutely no teeth.'

'I would die for you,' Kinetikus looked at Lilliane.

The determination in his gaze excited her.

He moved closer, and sat down opposite her, his eyes penetrating hers deeply.

She felt a tingling sensation running through her body.

'Close your eyes.'

Lilliane felt his lips resting gently on her eyes, travelling slowly but purposefully to her lips. Her mouth welcomed his, happy to greet her lover in a slow lingering kiss.'

Kinetikus closed his eyes. His hands became his eyes. He touched her, like a blind artist touches his chosen muse before painting her. Following the outline of her collar bone with his fingertips, moulding his hands gently around her shoulders and soft arms. Lilliane closed her eyes and felt his hands brushing over her alert breasts. She took a deep breath in. Her breasts were rising, magnetically drawn to his hands. He left them drowning in anticipation, and moved further to her hips and thighs. His hands went on the ultimate journey of discovery. They were fearlessly scouring the earth, in search of a deeply buried diamond. Kinetikus felt the energy of love rising between them. Her body became fluid in his hands. He slowly undressed her, until she was in her underwear. He could smell her sweet inviting scent.

"Lie down in the tent and keep your eyes closed," he said with gentle authority.

Lilliane waited for a short while, her heart was pounding when she realised, that he was taking his clothes off. She felt

93

the heat of his body as he lay next to hers. He continued to slowly undress her gently, until she was completely naked. His hands were now touching her bare skin. Slowly caressing and circling …tickling and teasing …stroking and squeezing… pulling and pinching softly. She gasped when they brushed over her pubic hair. He followed the outline of her soft hot inner thighs. She was melting into his touch. *I am liquid love.* His left hand was getting acquainted with her breasts, and his tongue was again dancing with hers, when she felt a surge of pleasure invading her body. His finger had scanned over her most sensitive spot. It was no accident and it returned, leaving just enough time, before her breath was taken away, for the second time. This time further fingers playfully joined in and showed no sign of mercy. They were on a mission to please.

'I will examine you,' Kinetikus said softly.

She felt a delicious sensation as he opened her gently with his fingers. *He is looking closely at me.* She felt his warm breath.

'I love being exposed to you in this way,' she whispered between breaths.

'You have beautiful teeth,' he joked.

Her laughter turned into a surprised moan, when she felt his finger entering her with no other intention than to cause her body to spontaneously experience sensual turmoil. She felt him everywhere in every way at the same time. He continued a relentless flowing motion of filling and emptying, teasing and pressing. Lilliane felt her energy rise to a distinctively high plateau.

'Please make love to me now,' she sighed.

His wet fingers slowly took her own hand, and lovingly directed it to continue in spontaneous play. She heard him preparing for love, and opened her eyes to see him fully.

What a beautiful man. He is my god, my king and divine

lover.

Her mouth opened in a soft moan, when she felt him against her.

Lilliane longed to be entered by him.

Being filled slowly, she collapsed into complete surrender. No thought could pervade the firewall of her senses anymore. She opened ever deeper into his loving embrace. Their bodies instinctively and effortlessly moved in a divine dance. They embarked on a joyful journey of gently rising and falling energy. Whenever he felt her arousal reach a high point, he settled the dance, allowing her energy to rest, before continuing to spiral it upwards. Lilliane could feel the point, at which her body would cease to be hers and begin to completely merge with his. She looked at him and he knew. He loved her deeper and stronger, more passionately than any man ever had. Like a volcano Lilliane erupted into gushing screams, tears and laughter. Shock wave after shock wave of pleasure was shaking her very foundations. He continued to move inside her. As she felt him joining her in ecstasy, she exploded into light. Together they entered a realm beyond time and space. Eternity sealed their union, as they lay in silent bliss.

*

Lilliane woke up with a long noisy yawn and was looking for her lover. The man, who had allowed her to become a woman.

Kinetikus was sitting in front of the tent, reading his book. He put the book down, lovingly stroked her cheek, and bent down to kiss her.

'Stop it, I need to go to the loo. I can't go if I am all wet and aroused. Keep your hands off me.'

He laughed, and heard her go into the bathroom, brush her teeth and sit down on the toilet.

She always leaves the door open. She does not seem to care about privacy when she is in the bathroom.
Kinetikus rushed into the room and started kissing her. She was caught off guard and protested.
'Can I wipe your front?' he asked.
'Hmm, are you worshipping my sacred gateway?'
'Indeed, I am.'
He very gently dabbed her with toilet paper, and Lilliane could feel her energy rise again.
Opening the tap for a shower, she climbed in the bathtub and let the water wet her hair and body. She closed her eyes and began shampooing her hair. Humming a slow melodic tune, Lilliane entered her inner world, enjoying the hot water on her body. The shower gel smelled fresh and invigorating, and her nose received her favourite essential oils with gratitude. Her hands were washing her body in respectful appreciation. The night had rendered it holy. Bending down for her loofah, she suddenly felt a rude and ribald finger entering her bottom unashamedly. She contracted in surprise, breathed into the strange and pleasurable experience, relaxed and opened to receive his finger fully.
Her female mouth began to water in sweet suspense. Lilliane pulled Kinetikus into the shower. His soaking boxer shorts stuck to his masculine backside and she could see the outline of his rising prowess. He pulled his shorts down, while she rubbed a little shower gel in her hands and began to wash him with care. Stroking and squeezing gently, she was pleased to notice his strong response to her touch. He kissed her with force, and she knew that his desire had grown beyond control. She knelt down, opened her mouth, and welcomed him deeply. His soft, smooth skin sliding gracefully beyond her inviting lips, her tongue woke up to the delights of a new delicious flavour. *I want to be filled by you.*

Lilliane's mouth grew more passionate, ready to receive him fully and completely, as he bent forward and reached around her back again. She moaned, when she felt his finger pushing deeply inside her. Her own finger was bathing in her sweet juices, surrendering to her deepest desire to be utterly filled by loving excited flesh. Shudders raged through their bodies, as they held onto each other free falling into nirvana.

*

'All I can think about is sex with you,' Lilliane sighed. 'How could I have lived my life without this? You have woken up the woman in me. I feel like a goddess, my body has become a temple of pleasure. Its divine purpose is solely to open into love and receive your gift for me. I have never felt more complete in my life. No work, achievement, accolade, title, project, art, learning experience or any other activity even comes close to this. It's the ultimate fulfilment I have longed for all my life. I did not know until now that I have been driven in a relentless search for it. A search for love. I've never had enough. I was looking for it in food, in relationships, movies, my studies, philosophy, art, romantic books…everywhere. However much I surrendered into the experience, even lost myself in it, the fulfilment did not last and the feeling of emptiness returned.

When you make love to me I feel so full, filled with love. The love continues to grow inside me and my heart expands. It has no boundaries.'

Lilliane's expression turned into pain.

'What are you feeling, Beautiful?'

'I feel so vulnerable, so afraid.' She began to cry. 'I am afraid of loosing you, my happiness depends on you.'

'You ARE already all the love that you seek, and you have experienced yourself as such, many times before. Like so many others you have only forgotten momentarily, and you feel you have to continue to search for a phantom. It is not my love that you have been looking for all your life; it is your own full expression of the love that is already within you. You will always feel this love, especially when you express it, and I will be the happiest man on earth to continue receiving it for as long as you desire to give it to me freely.'

'I love you more each day that it aches. I am so open, you could walk right into my heart and hurt me like no other.'

She continued to cry, and confessed through tears,

"Yesterday, in the restaurant, I felt your energy leave me. It was only for a brief moment when your attention was drawn to the waitress. She was very beautiful and feminine. While you ordered your meal, you smiled at each other, and I felt that I would die, that I had lost you. '

She sobbed in despair.

Kinetikus held her gently and allowed her tears to flow.

He said calmly, 'Love comes in countless shapes. There is the love you feel for a child and the love of your friends and family. The love of life and the whole universe, the unbounded love within you for all creation including yourself. The kind of love that we misunderstand the most, is really the simplest, most instinctive and spontaneous of all. What we perceive to be the most passionate expression of love between lovers, is based solely on every being's natural response to the opposing poles of the masculine and feminine energy. The feminine receives the masculine, and the masculine gives to the feminine. This attraction is a universal law for humans, animals, and even things. Like magnets, a feminine woman and a masculine man attract each other. You are a very feminine woman, and my masculine energy responds to you strongly. I will also naturally be attracted to the vibration of other feminine expressions. This is not only limited to women. My masculine pole can be drawn to the feminine pole of my environment. A flowing river, or a sensual soft meadow full of colourful flowers, is very enchanting, for example. I have witnessed your instinctive response to masculine energy in people and objects many times before. It is a sign of your feminine essence, and I cherish it as such. I do not fear losing you. I understand that, as long as we create natural polarity between us, our love and friendship will elevate this basic energy of attraction to a divine act of intimate communion. It is then completely unique and unrivalled and offers the deepest connection for not only our bodies, but also our souls. When I become aware of another very feminine woman, a natural attraction between two poles takes place. It is the same energy that attracts me so strongly to you.

'Although I cherish the sweet feminine in everything, I have no desire to act upon this type of attraction as I know that my ultimate freedom and fulfilment lies in experiencing your very own fullest expression of opening into intimate love with me.'

Lilliane looked impressed, somewhat relieved and contemplative.

'But, what happens if polarity dwindles? Isn't this the case with so many couples? Their relationship grows stale and both are, either secretly or overtly looking for sexual stimuli outside their relationship?'

'Contrary to common belief, polarity, or some people call it chemistry, does not simply *happen* to us. We either consciously or subconsciously create it with our being. Once we are aware of our own sexual essence, masculine or feminine, we can actively animate the feminine or masculine within us. Every person has both the masculine and the feminine essence but their natural resting point will tend towards cither one of these poles. Most men are more masculine at their core and most women are more feminine. A lot of women have learnt to animate their masculine side to such an extent, that men feel either compelled to compete or repulsed by them. It can be detrimental for any passionate relationship between partners to rest in poles that are not their natural cores. Sadly, women who are resting in their animated masculine side in a relationship, will unwillingly activate their partners' more feminine side. Often you find women who are deeply disappointed with the lack of focus, direction and masculine energy in their partner. They complain about their weakness and don't realise that they are co-creating this imbalance. The struggle for equality can diminish polarity as couples become more and more alike in their sexual energies. If polarity is lost over long periods of time, some relationships can be damaged severely. On the other hand, a masculine man who stays centred in his core, will naturally bring out the feminine in his woman, and the other way round. 'Every woman can cultivate her feminine core by spending more time in feminine environments and through such activities as dancing, or meeting with her feminine girlfriends. A man can do the opposite and activate his masculine directional energy through goal oriented work, martial arts or male masculine company, for example. This does not mean, that a woman can not have a career in a male world for example, but at the end of the day, both partners consciously have to allow themselves to relax into their natural sexual cores, if they wish to maintain a healthy and fulfilling intimate relationship.

'It is easy to create polarity, once you are aware of its dynamics. Growing deep unconditional love, trust and understanding can be much more of a challenge, yet a lot of people confuse polarity with love and move from affair to affair, hoping to find true love. Polarity is the strongest drive in nature, and vital for any intimacy between a woman and a man, but standing on its own, it can never lead to the deeply fulfilling love that we share.'

Lilliane looked at him in awe.

'I love you.'

'You are my woman.'

*

'What shall we do for New Years Eve?' Lilliane sounded excited.

Kinetikus looked amused.

'Lilliane, why don't we just decide on the night. I don't mind being among people but I would also enjoy spending the evening with you alone?'

Lilliane looked a little annoyed, at first, but then relaxed and began to smile.

'OK. No planning, hmmm? Agreed. The only thing I will make sure of, is that we have some nice food and champagne in the fridge.

I can't believe it is only 6 weeks until Christmas.'

'We will have known each other for almost a year in exactly 5 days.'

'What? Really? I don't remember the date of the conference. Yes, I guess it was around that time. I am impressed.'

Lilliane looked pensive.

Kinetikus smiled. He looked at her.

'I would love to cook for you at my place, if you like.'

Her eyes lit up. 'Excellent.'

*

It had been a while since Lilliane was at his flat. She felt a subtle nervousness and was clutching three orange roses and a small present for Kinetikus.

She rang the door bell.

'It's open.' Kinetikus voice sounded a little distorted.

She climbed up the stairs, and smelled a familiar mix of Mediterranean spices.

Kinetikus welcomed her at the door with a big grin on his face.

Lilliane took one look at him and burst out into laughter.

He wore loose fitting blue jeans and a black silk bow tie. Nothing else. His chest was completely bare and Lilliane rescued the Orange Lily that was trapped between his teeth.

'Well, hello.'

'Good evening, Milady, dinner will be served soon. May I guide you into the dining room.'

Every time Lilliane looked at him, she laughed. She noticed his bare feet.

'Sir, may I say, you are an excruciatingly attractive and remarkably hmm, yummy host? I am particularly drawn to your unique style of attire.'

'We aim to please.'

He vanished into the kitchen.

Lilliane leaned back on the sofa and listened to some Jazz coming from a CD player. The room fused with the flickering candles on the beautifully set table. She breathed in all his kind attention to detail and the scent of love.

Kinetikus walked in with a tray. A prawn cocktail and mixed leaf salad were gently placed in front of her.

Lilliane smiled in recognition.

About a year ago he had prepared the same meal for her and she had felt overwhelmed and afraid of his loving care.

This time she was savouring every millisecond. Nothing could overwhelm her anymore.

Kinetikus joined her, and they were enjoying their meal without the need for idle words. Many smiles and giggles escaped, hands were softly caressed and a series of seductive glances exchanged.

Let this moment last forever.

The Orange and Elderflower Sorbet was cooling Lilliane's palate, when Kinetikus placed a big envelope in front of her. She opened it and looked at him confused.

'These are descriptions of properties. Do you need my advice for work?'

He smiled.

'Which house do you like the most?' he asked.

'They are all lovely but I particularly like this one.'

'Would you like to be my permanent guest in it?' he asked.

'Are you moving?'

'I want to live with you, Lilliane. Let's move in together. We will save a fortune on phone bills,' he smiled.

She looked at him. Her eyes welled up, she felt overwhelmed for the second time.

Her expression gradually changed to an elated smile.

'Do you promise, that you will regularly cook for me in exactly this outfit?'

'I do.'

'OK, I'll think about it.'

'I will buy the house for us, and you can keep your place and rent it out, if you like.' Kinetikus continued.

'Are you sure this is what you want?' Lilliane looked at him.

'Absolutely.'

She reached for her bag and gave Kinetikus a small square present.

Kinetikus opened it and took out the CD that was inside.

It read "SACRED LOVE".

*

Lilliane was surprised to see Kinetikus waiting for her outside the airport arrivals gate. She had not expected him. It was a regular working day for him and he had told her that he had a meeting in the morning.

Kinetikus was still slightly out of breath: 'The meeting was cancelled. I just made it here. How was your trip? How is your family? God, I missed you.'

'Shut up and kiss me.' Lilliane pressed against him.

He felt his thoughts leaving his brain and his blood wielding the sceptre. They merged in a kiss. The airport noises disappeared as their lips and mouths welcomed each other with renewed curiosity.

Lilliane seemed restless.

'I am so horny. I have been thinking about you all the way back on the plane, and was contemplating having some fun on my own but now that you are here...we can just find a private spot somewhere.'

'Here, at the airport?'

'Why not?'

Kinetikus smiled. It was unusual for Lilliane to suggest this, as she generally preferred a more romantic setting. He scanned the airport and noticed a sign to the shower rooms.

'We can go over there, and lock the door,' he suggested.

Lilliane was already rushing towards her target, and he grabbed her hand when he caught up with her.

The shower room was clean, and fully tiled with three individual empty showers with screens.

Kinetikus pulled Lilliane in one of the cubicles and pressed her against the wall. She opened to his kiss while he lifted up her skirt and pulled down her panties. His finger reported with delight that her arousal was no figment of imagination but a tangible fluid reality. Her body was ready for him. He turned her around, and slowly entered her from behind. A soft moan escaped Lilliane's mouth. She threw her head back leaving her neck fully exposed. Gently kissing and biting her neck he stroked her back firmly through her soft silky blouse. His hands grabbed hold of her buttocks as his thrusts accelerated. Lilliane loved being filled by his masculine force. She was leaning against the wall, with both of her hands supporting her weight. Kinetikus lowered his pace and she knew that he was near the point of no return.

'Go for it, don't wait for me,' she whispered and immediately felt a deliciously deep and forceful thrust filling her whole being.

She closed her eyes and surrendered to his pleasure. *There is nothing like a strong man completely abandoning himself inside my body.*

Kinetikus shook against her as a wave of energy left his body.

Lilliane smiled at him.

*

He took her suitcase and signalled his driver. They cuddled on the backseat of the luxury car. Kinetikus detected a slight tension. Lilliane was silent.

'Lilliane, what are you feeling?'

She looked at him. Her expression revealed frustration.

'I don't want to spoil it for you,' she said. 'I had a great time just now, but it......it was not as fulfilling as the other times we made love. The position did not allow me to reach a climax easily and I could not use my hands because I would have banged my face against the wall. My legs got a bit tired. I hate standing up anyway and ...'

'And?'

'I am still aroused.'

He smiled amused, and stroked her hair gently.

'Thank you for being honest.'

Lilliane continued: 'On the plane I imagined how we would make love, and how it would be as absolutely perfect as the first time. I got so greedy. All I wanted was an orgasm. When I saw you, I was full of lust and, I guess, I just wanted to use your body. I really enjoyed feeling you inside me but I felt a little envious and disappointed that it seems easier for you to reach a climax. All these thoughts kept popping up in my mind; that it was not such a good idea to have sex at the airport after all; that it was a cold and ugly place for a sacred union. The more I tried to enjoy myself, the more it seemed out of my reach. I wanted it to be special because we have not seen each other for two whole weeks, and I missed your touch so much. Why couldn't I just enjoy myself as I did before? I feel like a failure, and that I have let you down.'

Tears were filling her eyes.

Kinetikus looked pensive.

'I never felt let down by you. Quite the opposite, I was very touched when I realised that you gave yourself in love and allowed me to focus on my own pleasure completely. I had a wonderfully wild time and felt deeply connected to you. To me an orgasm is not the goal, but a possible delightful gift at the end, and sometimes even at the beginning of a loving intimate encounter. Do you remember, when I said to you that we would make love in a hundred different ways? I meant it literally. I believe, that we make love every single day. We make love, when we look at each other, when you smile at me and touch my arm or hand. I make love to you with my voice, and when I share the air that you just exhaled. Every day we fill a big cup with love and when we have sex, it's because the cup is overflowing and the energy seeks to be transformed. Every intimate experience is unique. I choose not to judge one over the other. Such experience can be sacred, romantic, sensual, playful, funny, primal, predatory, desperate and a combination of all of these or more, yet they are all divine expressions of love. When I make love to you, I experience the moment, I am fully present in my body. You might have focussed solely on an orgasm as your desired outcome.'

'I was in my head again,' Lilliane sighed.

'Sometimes, if I have a thought distracting me from my

experience during love making, I say inwardly "Thank you for sharing". I then ask myself instead how does this *feel* in my *body*? This brings me straight back out of my mind into my body. Be gentle with your mind, it is no enemy, just a fearful child, that can be directed in a playful manner. Also it is important to be honest about what you enjoy or don't enjoy. Just because we started to be intimate in a certain manner, does not mean we have to take it the whole way. Always be true to your feelings.'

'So, you are not disappointed with me?' Lilliane asked.

'No, absolutely not.'

'Do you think, you could touch me now in the car?' Lilliane whispered excitedly.

Kinetikus used his long trench coat as a blanket, and opened her skirt.

She was still moist. 'It's like a furnace between your thighs,' he laughed.

'Ugh, your hands are cold!' she screeched.

The driver turned around curiously.

They stared out of the window with badly rehearsed blank expressions, laughter bubbling beneath the surface.

Lilliane leaned backwards and closed her eyes. She remained fully in her body, and relished the gentle motion of the limousine which perfectly complemented the exquisitely joyful ride.

*

The car was now parked outside her flat, and the driver began to unload her suitcase while she hastily adjusted her skirt.

Back in her lounge she hugged him and said: 'Thank you for making love to me in the car.'

'The pleasure was all mine.'

Lilliane looked annoyed. 'Oh no, I am starving, and there is no food in the fridge. Its not fair for you to take me out to eat all the time. So I guess, I'll have to go to the supermarket and get some soup and bread, or something really simple to prepare. I also need a few other items.'

She began to make a list.

'I don't like wasting our valuable time together buying food,' she huffed.

Her face suddenly lit up.

'I've got an idea. If we go off to shop together for the same items, it is such a waste of time. Why don't we split the shopping list in half, and have a race? That way we could get out of the supermarket in no time.'

Kinetikus smiled. 'You are on.'

Now that shopping had become a game instead of a chore, Lilliane beamed with energy. She went through the list.

'We will each have three items. To make it more interesting let's take on one extra task. We'll have to pick one fresh item from the bakery counter for each other. So you have to think about what I would like to have for a dessert and I'll pick something for you. Whoever makes it back to the car first is the winner.'

'What is the prize?' Kinetikus asked.

The winner will receive a sensual massage.

'I will be happy to win or lose with either outcome.' Kinetikus smiled.

Driving to the supermarket, Lilliane was feverishly considering a strategy to win, while Kinetikus sat with his eyes closed.

They entered the supermarket, and each took a basket.

'OK, Go!' Lilliane shouted, and rushed off giggling loudly.

They bumped into each other a couple of times amid fits of laughter.

Lilliane had collected her three items and approached the bakery counter.

I think I am ahead. I have done it very quickly. He is nowhere

in sight.
She impatiently waited for the assistant behind the counter to finish serving another customer. *Come on.*
'Yes, please!' The assistant took her order.
'Hmm, I would like one of the apple tarts please. No need to put it in a box, paper will do, thank you.'
As she received her apple tart, Kinetikus approached behind her and was awaiting his turn. She smiled at him, certain of her victory.
'I'll wait for you by the car! Please get me the apricot tart!' she chirped in a patronising pitch and ran off to the nearest cashier.
She quickly checked which cashier near her had the smallest queue and picked one with only one shopper in front of her. *Come on.*
Lilliane kept an eye on the other tills. He was nowhere in sight.
She ran outside to the car.
Kinetikus was leaning against her car, demonstratively checking his watch.
She was outraged, and shouted while laughing, '*How* did you *do* that? I was in front of you and I checked the other tills.'
They got into the car.
Kinetikus was catching his breath. *At least he had been running too.*
'This has been an amazing experience. I learnt so much about myself,' he said. 'I did not have a specific strategy but visualised me winning before our race began. When I saw you running off, I realised that I did not even know what items were on my list nor where to locate them in relation to my position. You, on the other hand, seemed to know exactly where to go. I picked up the items as they were on the list, time was too short to work out which order would be the most efficient. I did not run but walked in a steady fast pace

and left the bakery counter until last. When I saw you there, I realised that I was behind. I love seemingly impossible challenges so I felt compelled to come up with a winning strategy quickly. I saw you running to the nearest till from the bakery counter but noticed, to my delight, that the exit of the supermarket was at the opposite far end of the row of tills. I ran as quickly as I could across the back of the aisles and joined the fast check-out queue nearest to the exit. It had just become free when I arrived. I saw you looking around at the other end. You did not notice me as you were only checking the tills nearest you.'

'I can't believe it! I was ahead of you.' Lilliane sighed and accepted her defeat. She said in a contemplative tone, 'I had a strategy before we entered the supermarket and felt prepared, though not overly confident or certain of my victory; but I was up for a good laugh and a challenge. I had thought about the location of the items and which would be the fastest way to pick them on my way to the bakery counter. When we began the race, my adrenaline got the better of me and I ran to a completely random item. I realised that I had actually disregarded my own strategy. I had to rush back to fetch the first item according to my plan. Remember, when we bumped into each other again? I took a deep breath and re-focussed on my goal while keeping up my pace. After that it went very well. When I realised you were behind at the bakery counter, I relaxed and felt certain of my victory. I stopped focusing and actually lost my momentum. This is astonishing. You are the tortoise and I am the hare. I can't believe, I lost. If I had stayed focused until the end, I could have won.'

'I have identified where I did well, and where I could improve,' Kinetikus said.

'You won, why do you need to improve anything?'

'You can always improve something. How you do **anything,**

is how you do **everything**. He who knows others is learned. He who knows himself is wise. I believe that the biggest opportunities we have to look at our behaviour are exactly those occasions when, either in real life or in this case through a game, the heat is turned up and we find ourselves in a challenging or stressful situation. For example, I did well on trusting that I would win, stayed flexible and confident enough to adopt a quick new strategy at the crucial point, and also multiplied my speed at the end. However, I can certainly improve on my initial strategy, and particularly my overall speed, while maintaining my trust, flexibility and focus.'

'Amazing, I can really see my pattern of responding to stress,' she laughed. 'I lost my head, and my strategy was out of the window.'

'Remember, to observe what you did *right* first,' he laughed.

She looked at him. 'I did well to establish a good strategy before the race, understood the importance of speed and acted accordingly. I showed a degree of flexibility when I calmed down after my initial panic and re-focused on the challenge. However, my initial response to stress was fearful; so my emotions cancelled my strategy and I wasted time and energy because of it. When I became aware of my advantage, my Ego took over. I felt certain of my victory, and actually saved you time, while wasting my own valuable seconds by telling you which tart I wanted! After all, it was supposed to be your task to pick one for me. Overall, my finishing was very poor. From now on, I will keep to my strategy, speed and flexibility, but stay calm and focused until the very end of the challenge. I will be aware but not distracted by what others are up to, whether they seem to be behind or ahead. It does not mean anything. We all focus too much on where others are at and we judge ourselves by comparing ourselves to others, either positively or negatively. Ultimately, it does not matter so much where we are but in which direction we are going.'

'Amazing how fifteen minutes of shopping can help you to become aware of so much. I've got one question for you,' Kinetikus added.

'Yes?'

'How much did it matter to you to win?'

'Hmm, that's a very good question. It felt very important to me, I think, that's one of the reasons why I lost my head. Although it was just a game, I did not like the idea of losing. I can feel like a failure if I lose at what I considered is easily achievable. What about you?'

'I feel that I am always gaining something whether I win or loose. That's why, ultimately, I do not mind. It's also much easier to keep one's cool, if one is less fixed on a result. My goals tend to manifest more effortlessly, I find, the more specific I am in my choices and the more detached I am from the outcome.'

'Thank you for playing with me.' Lilliane said softly and parked the car outside the house.

Later during their meal, she teased him. 'You know, of course, that I am a much faster learner than you and that it will be impossible to beat me at our next supermarket race.'

'This is the kind of healthy competition I like,' he laughed. 'I accept your challenge. In the meantime, I look forward to my sensual massage.'

'It will be my pleasure to serve you tonight,' she said in a velvety voice.

*

Lilliane had bought fireworks for New Year's Eve. The Festive Season had come and gone and the taste of Christmas was still occupying the cell memory of her taste buds.

Kinetikus cooked the dinner for their spontaneous New Year's Eve.

Lilliane was annoyed with herself for not fully appreciating his culinary efforts. She had harboured secret hopes for a grander way to celebrate New Years Eve. They had made absolutely no plans and they would not be able to go to any organised party. In addition, she had declined two invitations from friends to keep the evening open.

She put on a brave face and smiled at him.

'What's wrong?'

'I don't know what we could do to celebrate. I have never stayed at home on New Year's Eve.'

'We don't have to stay home. There are a number of bars and pubs that we could go to. I am open to anything.'

'OK. After our meal let's go out. I feel like some fresh air. I'll change into something a little more dressy and we can try out some places within walking distance. There is one bar that's quite nice.'

Lilliane looked a little happier now that they had a vague plan.

Much later they were still wandering the streets in search of a suitable venue. Her feet were beginning to hurt, and she could feel disappointment rising.

All the places they tried needed to be booked in advance.

They had passed one bar that looked OK on the way but decided to look further.

'Let's go back and see if we can still get into that last place. It's better than nothing,' Lilliane said defeated.

The bar was smoky and crowded, the music so loud that they had to shout into each others ears. Kinetikus pushed through the people to the bar and ordered two drinks. It was only forty-five minutes until midnight. Admittedly, he had thought it easier to find a venue. Neither of them was in a particular party mood after walking in the cold for so long.

Lilliane collapsed on the armrest of a crowded leather sofa. *I need to defrost. My feet are hurting. What am I doing here?*

113

Kinetikus brought the drinks and Lilliane was happy to sip on her hot drink.

'I'll be back in a minute,' she said heading for the cloakroom.

Lilliane looked at herself in the mirror.

Come on cheer up, I am in love with a gorgeous man who is going to live with me. I don't need to dream about a Cinderella style New Year's Eve. It's the prince that matters, not the Fairytale Ball. I can have fun in a grotty, smoky bar instead. She smiled. *It's just a few hours to the rest of my life. We can dance for a while and observe the hypocrisy of this mad scheduled frenzy. Everybody is in the same boat. I have never seen so many forced smiles as on New Year's Eve.*

Two pretty girls in extremely revealing outfits came into the toilets.

How can anyone look for love in an outfit like this, I fail to understand.

Lilliane suddenly felt overcome with gratitude. *I have absolutely no reason to be miserable.*

She returned to the main room full of energy, only to freeze.

A very attractive and flamboyantly dressed woman was talking to Kinetikus. They seemed familiar with each other.

Her hand was resting on his shoulder and her face was in close proximity to his. *She is obviously not interested in his views on politics.*

Lilliane felt a stabbing pain in her stomach, and could not get herself to move. She was watching the scene from a distance, and now the woman whispered something into Kinetikus' ear. He laughed.

Lilliane was in agony.

Kinetikus spotted her and sensed her pain.

He walked over to her.

'Lena is an old colleague of mine. She has just split up with her partner and is a little drunk. No need to take her

behaviour seriously.'
'Great, we can celebrate New Year's Eve together. I have always dreamt of a threesome.' Lilliane felt exhausted. Midnight came and went. While the crowd went mad, Lilliane sat in a corner and watched a drunken woman attempting to dance with her boyfriend.

*

Twenty minutes into the New Year, they were walking back home without talking.
'That has been the worst New Year's Eve of my life,' Lilliane broke the silence.
'It's not my fault if somebody expresses an interest in me.' Lilliane could hear frustration in Kinetikus' voice.
'Lilliane. You are the only one for me. At no point, during the evening, was there any threat to our relationship and yet you behave as if I have committed adultery.'
'She was all over you. She even kissed you on your neck.'
'We cannot control the outer game but we can change the inner game. If women make advances to me without respecting you, that does not have to be an unpleasant experience. It, ultimately, has nothing to do with us. I have witnessed a lot of guys who were very attracted to you, some of them were more respectful than others. I don't blame you for it.
Why should anyone have any impact on our New Years Eve at all? Let's not dwell on what happened, and just enjoy the rest of the night together.'
Lilliane felt defeated. She knew he was right.
They arrived at her flat and she remembered the fireworks that she had bought as a surprise.
'Let's blow up my garden,' Lilliane smiled. 'Would you like to light some serious rockets?' she asked Kinetikus.
'I have watched many firework displays but, apart from a

115

few firecrackers, I have never actually lit anything myself,' he admitted.

'Great, there is always a first for everything. I love firsts. It's really easy. As children, my brother and I used to be real pyromaniacs and on New Years Eve, we always had fireworks in our garden. Let's take turns. You can light a rocket and then I will. I bought a huge box.'

I can see that.

Lilliane went to the fridge and poured two glasses of champagne. She handed one to Kinetikus and raised the other.

'I henceforth forgive any woman who feels attracted to my man. I thank you for reminding me of my blessings and impeccable taste.'

She continued, 'This is a special toast to everyone who believes in love. May you never give up or settle for second best.'

She looked pensive. 'I've got an idea. Let's put out a positive intention with each rocket that hits the sky.'

'Great, that's my girl.'''

For the next forty-seven minutes the sky, above the urban back garden, blasted light in a riot of blazing colours. With each explosion a deep prayer was catapulted into the starlit universe. Specific intentions, bundled like laser beams, passed planets and galaxies and travelled faster than the speed of light. Every single one reached their destination in an instant.

*

Lilliane was awake, and wrote in her diary:

I love being proved wrong. What I thought was a terrible New Year's Eve celebration turned into a magical night.
We had so much fun lighting fireworks in my little garden. I did not miss the crowds at all. I understand now that I

adopted a manufactured concept of how this night should be celebrated. I've given up yet another subconscious treadmill. We look back at the riches of our past, and we look forward to a future of choice and loving action. But I feel at my most grateful for the time in between, when we are completely in the present, and we let our bodies feel and express love in the unique and exquisite moment of the now.

There is a divine lover in everybody. I have chosen to nurture my divine lover, while observing my ego-lover with growing compassion. Divine Lovers make mistakes and encounter challenges. These are vital ingredients for growth. They learn not only to accept, but to truly welcome these challenges. The only difference, between Ego-Lovers and Divine Lovers, is that one acts out of fear and the other out of love. Fear is stucknesss and love is flowingness.

Divine lovers can be fearful of losing each other at times but they know this fear to be a trick of their mind and do not allow it to control them. They see their partner's boundless creative potential, and desire nothing more, than to witness each other break through limitations and grow. They do not choose to limit, cage or restrain each other in any way. Trusting that they were meant to make this journey together, they accept the possibility of having to step aside, if their partner chooses to travel alone. While their hearts aches at the thought of this, their souls always rest in oneness.

The level at which I choose to love, determines the level of the lover I attract. I attract exactly what I need to grow. Every moment is divine perfection. It is OK to be an Ego-Lover one day, and a Divine Lover the next. I am an Ego-Lover until the moment I no longer choose to be one.

Lilliane was shopping, and gently squeezed a couple of avocados to test their ripeness. Leaving the supermarket, she caught the eye of a middle aged woman standing near the exit. She was handing out flyers for the local adult education centre. Lilliane felt invigorated by her warm smile. She took a leaflet, and realised to her surprise, that the venue was within walking distance from the house. On her way home, Lilliane felt compelled to take a detour, and visit the centre. She was not sure, what she was looking for, took a brochure listing all the available classes, and began to flick through the pages. *Maybe an aerobics class or yoga. I would like to do something physical. I am in my head more often than necessary.* Her thoughts were interrupted by laughter. A group of four voluptuous women entered the centre. They looked, as if they had just attended an Arabian Nights costume ball. As they purposefully opened one of the nearby doors, Lilliane could hear exotic music coming from inside the room.

'Excuse me, what kind of class are you attending?' she shouted.

'Advanced belly dancing, it's great fun.' They disappeared into the room.

Lilliane felt a surge of excitement in her body. It had decided for her.

*

She could hear his key in the door. Lilliane felt a sense of anticipation in the evening, before he came home from work. *I can't believe, I have been living with him for five months. It seems so unreal.* Stirring a risotto, she heard him enter the house. Her heart began to beat and she impatiently counted the seconds until she could feel his soft lips on the back of her neck. He turned her around and they stood in a firm silent embrace.

We are eternally one.
She stroked his wind-cooled face and looked at him as if she had to remind herself of his features. The morning seemed a long time ago.
'Thank you for being in my life.' She looked at him, and lit a candle on the table.
'Thank *you*, Beautiful.'
Kinetikus started dishing the food.
'May this food bless our minds, bodies and souls,' Lilliane said.
They began their meal and enjoyed eating in silence for a little while.
'I have to leave in about 40 minutes,' Lilliane said a little hesitatingly. 'I've enrolled in a dance class.'
'Excellent' What kind of dance?' Kinetikus asked.
'Hmm, it focuses on exercising the abdominal area and upper thighs.'
Lilliane wanted to surprise him with a private dance when she felt ready, so she decided not to give full details of her new interest.
'As long as you enjoy it,' Kinetikus smiled at her.

*

Two hours later, a flushed and radiant looking Lilliane rang the door bell. Kinetikus opened the door.
'Excuse me Sir, are you interested in purchasing kisses for charity?'
He laughed surprised.
'I won't purchase any, but I am happy to donate one.'
They stood kissing at the door.
'You look as if you had a good time,' he commented.
'Oh, it was amazing. Lovely women. They were all very different and great fun. After an initial period of feeling a little self-conscious, everybody let their hair down. The

119

teacher is a real character.'

Lilliane wondered if she had given away too much, so she added,

'She showed us a simple dance routine which is a little like aerobics but coming more from the hips. I can't believe we danced for over an hour. I felt a little tired before I went but now I am full of energy. You know me. Normally I find these kind of workouts boring and they leave me exhausted. This is quite different.'

Kinetikus looked pensive.

'A while ago, I read that our physiology is one of the most powerful tools to change our states and energy levels. Whenever we are in a negative state, our body language inevitably matches the state. For example, we sit slouched with our heads facing down. When we feel low in energy and spirit, it might seem silly to consciously change our physiology but it has a powerful proven positive effect. It's difficult to be depressed when you are jumping up and down, or even lift your head up high to get a glimpse of the sky. Smiling is great, even if you don't really feel like it at the time. I believe dancing and singing are at the top of the list in releasing feel-good hormones in your body. Researchers are going as far as to say that it is often our physiology that causes our states, not the other way round. We are depressed and think that we therefore must keep our heads down. Yet it is keeping our heads down that will create a feeling of depression. We ARE not depressed! We DO depression but, more importantly, we can UNDO it. In a US study researchers repeatedly changed the physiology of clinically depressed patients in a mental institution. They had to smile and celebrate every day, and watch funny movies etc. After only a short period of time, 80% were permanently cured of depression without the use of any drugs. They had conditioned their nervous systems to a more resourceful pattern of physiology.'

Lilliane looked at him fascinated. She laughed.

'I think sex is a great way to create a healthy physiology. I don't mean love-less romping but fulfilling true intimacy. I feel lighter and energised after we've made love. It seems to be accumulative. My energy flows stronger after each time we've made love and I feel more alive. I feel our natural energy or life-force is actually the same as our sexual energy and it does not only express itself through sex but in any creative way. When we feel full of life, we are passionate about many things not only about the physical expression of love. I feel enthusiastic about so many things now; yet I remember a time when I envied people who had a deep interest or hobby. I didn't feel passionate about anything in my life. Our society does not really encourage passionate living either, not to mention full sexual expression. On the one hand, sex is openly shown and discussed everywhere in the media. Yet true intimacy still seems mostly a taboo. When I bring up the subject and talk about it openly, I am always surprised to find how many women are not sexually fulfilled or have lost their interest in sex completely.'

'They could take dancing lessons as a second option.' Kinetikus was only half serious.

'I agree with you that changing one's physiology is a powerful positive tool. It is equally important to allow ourselves to feel a deep emotion. We've learnt to suppress so regularly that many of us have forgotten how to feel a happy or unhappy emotion fully. But if a strong emotion is suppressed, it is stored as a toxic cell memory in the body and can eventually manifest as a physical pathology. It is much healthier to stay present, and allow oneself to completely feel an emotion when it arises. It can travel through one's body quite quickly. Emotion is nothing but energy in motion. Changing the physiology to change a negative state is helpful when that state is not due to a real core emotion. I think, we know pretty well, when our low mood is based on a story that we created in our mind or when it is based on real grief or anger. I sometimes witness myself going into a story and my ego can get a real kick out of feeling low and significant. Changing my physiology can be a great tool then but it requires radical honesty with myself. After all, I am that same person who created the story.'

*

Lilliane turned silent and looked outside the window at the enormous full moon. *I finally recognise the face of the man in the moon. When I stopped straining my eyes in search of him, he emerged effortlessly.*
Struggle is my great illusion.
Kinetikus felt instinctively drawn to her hips, unaware that they had been playing the lead role at her last dancing class. Standing close behind her, he slowly traced the curve that led from her waist over her hips. Lilliane felt a tingling trail of golden light entering her.
She looked at him. 'I always feel a little shy when I want to make love to you,' she confessed.
He smiled. 'It is a new experience every time. We open to each other afresh and are vulnerable.'
They embraced lightly.
Hearts connecting.
Lilliane closed her eyes.
I am home in his heart.
She felt his kisses leaving an invisible floating trail on her body. They were lingering in mid-air caressing tiny hairs standing on end.
Where will our love take us tonight?
His hands wandered over her naked glowing moonlit landscape as he embarked on the fearless brave journey of a

childlike explorer, bewildered by the unknown nature of the known.
A change in temperature so subtle that only innocence could notice it.
A difference in taste so minute that only an unspoilt tongue could welcome it.
A single skipped heart-beat that could be lost forever without a listening heart.
His body had taken the lead in their waltz and Lilliane let her body flow, turn and spin until she was dizzy with love. In his arms, the dizziness did not threaten her anymore. She welcomed the once scary stranger with open arms and told it to come and join her. The dizziness was unfamiliar with loving acceptance and took a couple of tiny baby steps until it dipped its toes into the ocean from where it had emanated. It giggled in the realisation that it had been afraid of itself, that the ocean was there to dive into, and that it had always been a great diver.
Lilliane felt a surge of energy lifting her body to take the lead.
Let me show you the glory of being lost.
He softly surrendered in his own receptive beauty and opened to the gift of being held in her dizziness.
He is so beautiful. So beautiful is he.
They danced and danced until she realised in a bright glimpse of awe that he was no longer held by her. All - he, her and the dizziness - were held by the waltz itself. Its gravitational force had created a safe soft blanket for them to lean against. It was warm, tasted salty and felt a little oily on their skin. Weightlessly, they floated in the purest of electric crystal clear blue. When the three master divers emerged, the ocean smiled in love.
The dizziness returned to the ocean and left the two lovers gently washed ashore. Wise waves waved a warm goodbye.

Blazing sunlight pierced through the gaps between the curtains. Lilliane found her limbs entwined with his as she slowly entered her body after the journey of the night.

His hand said thank you to her thigh.

She slowly rose and walked naked into the kitchen where she poured a little mango juice in two glasses and diluted it with cold fresh water.

She fed him with the sweet juice and commanded in a strong, conspiratorial, yet vulnerable and slightly fearful voice.

'Tell me something about you that you have *never* told anybody else. Something that I might judge you for if I did not love you *completely*?'

Kinetikus looked at her.

'Are you sure?'

'Absolutely!'

He hesitated for a while. Lilliane knew that he already knew.

He began, 'Before I met you I was single for quite a while. I was mostly focusing on building and running my own business. On a number of nights, I stayed in the office until quite late and was so wide awake that I knew I would not be able to sleep, unless I found a way to distract and relax my mind. I started to go to late-night bars because they served drinks until the early hours. I got quite drawn into the openly sensual atmosphere of a few strip clubs. After a hard day at work, I would have a drink at one of the bars and calm my mind in a world that was so far away from my business affairs, that it was easy to forget about it. I found the energy in these places strangely relaxing. It was not about being aroused although that happened when a dancer felt very comfortable in her body. Some of the dancers began to trust me and sense that I was not looking at them as mere objects but, rather, with the gratitude of someone who receives a great gift. Very rarely I would order a private dance and, on one occasion, a dancer became so aroused that I allowed her to use my hand on herself.'

Lilliane's face displayed hurt and shock.

She looked in his eyes and saw his deepest fear.

Her heart opened as wide as the world.

She said slowly, "When I was twenty-one I was arrested for shoplifting. It had become an addiction. It was never about the goods. Only the thrill. The thrill of doing something that was dangerous and forbidden. I got more and more daring and started to play a game with the shop assistants, raising their suspicion and then, when I knew they had their eyes on me, I would steal things right under their eyes without them noticing. I guess, in a way, I wanted to be caught. I was on a ferry once and had stolen a very small item. I did not expect it to set off the alarm when I walked through the electronic barrier but it did. I was in shock when I realised that my game was over. On a ship, there is nowhere to run. I had to return to my departure port and was escorted by two armed police officers in front of a suspicious crowd. At the police station, they took my finger prints and asked me a whole lot of humiliating questions. After this incident, I had a criminal record for a couple of years until they struck me off the register.'

Kinetikus looked at her. He smiled.

'I knew you were a dangerously skilful thief when I realised you had stolen my heart yet I have no intentions of asking you to give it back!'

'That's because you have owned mine all along!'

*

Lilliane lay awake. Her mind was empty, yet her hands continued to write in her diary.

When I asked him to reveal his shadow-side to me, I had no idea what to expect. Initially, my judgement did have a

125

foothold in my heart. However, when I opened my heart so wide as to envelop all fear and pain, it swallowed the whole thorny bush and spat out a giant pristine Orange Lily instead. Then I knew at once that there can never be any shadow without the light that allows the shadow to exist. And I saw more and more of his light. I desired to merge with his body more than ever after he had shown this other self. What he calls polarity, I shall call the holy erotic force. The secret of this never-ending sacred desire lies not only in being my true feminine self but, more especially, in our constant growth, deepest exposure and revelation to each other. Our souls long for oneness. They need to connect and discover each other. We are mistaken to assume that we completely know certain aspects of ourselves and the other. Each soul has infinite facets that can only sparkle at exposure to light. In understanding our own soul to have endless, as yet unseen, depths, we can embark on a joyous and, at times, frightening journey of self-discovery and never-ending growth and, in doing so, we forever have gifts to reveal and share with the other. It is the purpose of my other half to bring to the surface all of my shadows, and this can be painful and frightening at times. All masks must fall. Yet all shadows that are discovered either within the self or within the other are purified together and so, every day, two new people meet afresh in love.

*

'Kinetikus,' Lilliane shouted enthusiastically, 'today I attended an illuminating lecture by an eminent speaker in the field of mind-body medicine. It's great to see so much scientific evidence for a truth that can be felt by anyone who listens deeply to their body and inner wisdom. The speaker illustrated the illusion of reality. Time and space are good examples of man-made references in an attempt to measure

126

the immeasurable. He referred to physical objects as **space-time events** and...'

Kinetikus interrupted her flow, 'You have got an amazing pair of space-time events!'

He observed in amusement how her focus gradually left her mind and entered the physical world.

She laughed. 'Normally, it is my purpose to bring you back from your directional, goal-oriented world into your body, and to enchant you.'

'Well, you have been doing exactly that just by your mere presence. I have been finding it difficult to concentrate on anything else tonight. You have a very sensual energy about you.'

She smiled. *I wonder if it has got anything to do with what I did today or maybe my secret passion. I have been studying belly dancing for quite a while now and he might sense it.*

'Well, why don't you begin to uncover the mystery by giving any one of my space-time events a closer inspection?'

It was a mild evening of the kind that awakens the spring in humans and animals alike. The large soft rug in the lounge had been delivered yesterday. After today's inspiring lecture, Lilliane had enjoyed a lingering bath and spent the rest of the afternoon lying on the new rug, reading a book on sensual massage. It had been very fulfilling to try out some of the described techniques on herself.

'I would like to give you a special massage.'

'Great, just what the Homeopath ordered.'

*

Lilliane closed her eyes, breathed in deeply, and let the energy of love flow through her until she could feel it as a continuous strong current warming her body and filling her heart. She saw it pouring from her hands, touching his skin and permeating his cells until it reached his inner organs.

127

Kinetikus felt himself relax deeper with every stroke of her hands and closed his eyes. He had anticipated a soft sensual touch and was surprised at the strength of her small hands slowly warming and waking up his body. She pressed, pulled and pinched slightly, at specific points on his sides and along his spine and continued her touch in circular movements all over his body. When she used only the pressure of her fingertips, followed by a soft flat stroke around his back and thighs, Kinetikus felt his energy rise and fall, slightly plateau, and then rise again until it reached a slightly higher point. He surrendered completely to the unfamiliar sensations in his body. A tingling sensation spread through his whole body and cleared his head of any traces of remaining thoughts. Her love fed his arteries and blood vessels, nourishing his organs and cells.

One by one, the circles inside his body began to chime and spin. Together, they sang a song of happiness. He felt the light growing stronger in his centre as her hands moved intimately, keeping a respectful distance that stirred longing. The stirring slowly spiralled upwards. She let it rest in confusion, before taking it a little further. Unaware that he was climbing, he innocently followed the enchanting tune of the flower. For a while the Lily let him rest by a clear mountain stream, be carried like a baby, meandering to his next stop, where they began a slow invisible ascent. The sun shone more intensely with every breath, until it broke out in a blinding blaze behind the tall mountain-top trees; invading, radiating through his whole body, drenching every cell up to his crown, leaving him in the most sublime bliss. His breathing ceased momentarily, while his inner breath carried him to a lake of total stillness. He bathed in the velvety purple light and dropped even deeper into the deepest silence.

Lilliane read through her diary.

Kinetikus and I were challenged today. A misunderstanding spiralled out of control and I verbally attacked him in rage. I learnt about an important key to freedom.

My Ego comes in many guises.

At the end of a disagreement cycle, when we have expressed ourselves and begin to feel a deeper understanding of each other, it can strike unpredictably.

I am at the point, where I have forgiven whatever was tied to my anger.

My Ego takes pride in my forgiveness and eagerly awaits to receive forgiveness too.

At that point, anger rises again if I am not forgiven according to my expectations.

But mine is the choice always.

The nature of Divine Love is unconditional.

I choose to forgive, regardless of whether I am forgiven.

That is my only way.

*

Lilliane glanced fervidly at Kinetikus who was resting on the bed, watching her undress.

I am overflowing with love. I wish for nothing more than to nurture, heal and enchant him and the world.

She undressed and stood naked in front of him.

Kinetikus observed her reaching inside her wardrobe. To his surprise, she pulled out an orange sparkly sequinned hip belt with hanging beads and coins, and wrapped it around her hips, leaving her belly button exposed. She pressed a button on her CD player.

She stood still, strong and centred in calm anticipation, her body ready to be taken on an exquisite journey of the senses. It was completely open to receive the vibration of the music. With the first note, Kinetikus witnessed in amazement, how

129

her hips began to flow very slowly in a sensual horizontal figure of eight. They were moved by an invisible force. His ears delighted in the scintillating, slow, tingling of countless beads and coins. Her arms opened into a fluid universal embrace while her hands were floating in soft caressing waves. Every part of her body was engaged in a symphony of continuous movement. It had no beginning and no end. She closed her eyes, inviting the music to fill every last cell of her body. The world around her ceased to exist as a separate entity. Like her own blood, the music coursed through her. A female body responding gracefully from a place of intrinsic beauty. Her flesh surrendered in the divine expression of unbounded love. Kinetikus was captivated, witnessing how her body gave rise to the mesmerising art of a dancing goddess.

I can feel her love. It is bigger than me, it is all encompassing.

He welcomed his tears.

The beat accelerated, and, with the sound of intermittent soft tribal drums now infusing the enchanting melody, her feminine soft belly slowly woke up to the vibrations. It gently breathed in and out in undulating caressing moves. Her hips continued to roll from side to side, blissfully taking turns with her now fully alive abdomen. The music accelerated further, and her hips, bottom and thighs were suddenly united in one shimming motion which was accentuated by rhythmical flicks. With the continuously rising beat, the centre of her body breathed in ever faster waves of ecstatic bliss, until her belly was fluttering in one big shiver of love. Her face became flushed. Her lips relaxed in a voluptuous open smile. She gasped and dove into ultimate surrender, her highest expression of divine love. Kinetikus witnessed her entire body shimmying and shaking, lapping and rolling, writhing and bending furiously, until she collapsed onto the floor in shudders of pleasure, broken by laughter and lubricated by tears of overflowing joy. A flood of energy was surging through his entire body and Kinetikus was left speechless and in awe.

*

'When I dance, I make love to the universe,' Lilliane whispered, catching her breath.
'When I make love, I dance with the universe.' Kinetikus replied smiling.
'They say Love is blind but it is Fear that is blind. Only Love can truly see.'

EPILOGUE:

Michael really enjoyed his birthday party. A lot of old friends had come to see him and the party had continued until the early hours. Back in his bedroom, contemplating the event, he felt vulnerable. It had only been two months since the end of his relationship. He looked at all his presents and began to open them. His older sister Sandrine had sent a small parcel from abroad. He admired his sister. She was very happy and loved her family and life. She talked openly about her past as a night club dancer to fund her studies at art college and she was now a passionate art-lecturer at a university.

Michael opened the wrapping paper and recognised the shape of a book. It had a golden hand on it. He smiled. *Sandrine always finds interesting literature.*

He looked outside and saw that the sun would be rising soon. He did not feel tired. Michael put on his coat and slid the book into his pocket.

*

The park was still asleep and only the birds were welcoming the day enthusiastically. He had never been to the park at this early hour and loved the clear fresh smell of the new dawn. Listening to his muffled footsteps on the grass, he took a different turn and noticed the entrance to another park. He could see a small church in the distance. Michael sat down on a bench, closed his eyes and soaked up the first rays of the rising spring sun.

He woke up to the sound of laughter. He saw a couple chasing each other around an old oak tree. They had not noticed him. He tried to estimate how old they were but he could not come to any conclusion. *They are ageless. Carefree like children. Is this the true face of love? Playfulness.*

They stopped the chase. The man walked towards the bench and sat down next to Michael, still catching his breath. He looked at him and nodded with an open warm smile. Michael felt his entire body relax. While the man's loving gaze was following the actions of the woman, who was preparing breakfast on a picnic blanket, Michael took out his new book and began to read.

The man took a deep breath in, and turned towards him. Pointing to the book, he said, 'It's a story about divine lovers.'

Michael looked at him in surprise.

The man smiled and said: **'A woman is breathing on this earth right now, drinking from the same pool of oxygen as you, who is designed for you by the heavens. She is someone so divinely matched for you, that were you to describe your deepest dreams and desires for a lover, friend and companion, and pour out your heart and soul filling countless pages, when you _come to fully recognise her_, you will know in a wave of gratitude that she exceeds all of this by a hundredfold.'**

Tears were in his eyes. '_Feel_ the _infinite love_ that resides in your very core, and her face will greet you in a sweet mirror of your own essence.'

Dear Reader,

Since completing the manuscript for Kinetikus I have
come across the following two books of great value to
both men and women. They address the issues of
feminine and masculine sexual energy, sacred intimacy
and the play between the masculine and feminine poles
in a practical and in-depth way, which complements the
lyrical nature of Kinetikus. I recommend them from the
bottom of my heart:

The Multiorgasmic Woman
Sexual Secrets every woman should know
By Mantak Chia and Dr. Rachel Carlton Abrams

The Way of the Superior Man
By David Deida

One simple book made a profound impact on myself
and comes recommended above all others for anyone
who chooses to consciously create all aspects of their
lives:

Ask and it is Given
Learning to Manifest Your Desires
By Ester and Jerry Hicks

Play life to the fullest!

With love

Susanne Meis

About the Author

Susanne Meis was born in Cologne, Germany. She lived in Paris and London, and has a professional background in Linguistics. In 2001 an experience profoundly changed the direction of her life. She has since become an enthusiastic advocate of Energy Medicine and Personal Growth, qualifying amongst others in Homeopathy, Neurolinguistic Programming and Journey Process Therapy. Susanne is passionate about life and LOVE and lives with her partner and daughter near London, United Kingdom.

For more information about the author and her work visit:

www.orangelily.org

KINETIKUS READERS' GIFT

If you wish to pass on Kinetikus to your loved ones, we are offering Kinetikus readers a Gift Discount on any further copies. To find out more, or take advantage of this opportunity, please go to:

www.orangelily.org

Printed in the United Kingdom
by Lightning Source UK Ltd.
115039UKS00002B/85-117